The deadliest terror of all . . .

"She's not just in our dreams anymore," Jessica said, her face creased with tension. "She's—she's in reality now." Her eyes stared straight ahead. Elizabeth could see a few beads of sweat appear on her sister's forehead. "She's here, and she's going to kill us in our beds, and—"

"No way." But even as Elizabeth spoke she felt her heart seize up with fear. Jessica's right, she told herself.

It was bad enough when the monster was only at the Riccolis'. And it was bad enough when she was only in their dreams. But if she's going to terrorize us at our house, when we're wide awake . . .

SWEET VALLEY TWINS

If I Die Before I Wake

Written by
Jamie Suzanne

Created by
FRANCINE PASCAL

BANTAM BOOKS
NEW YORK·TORONTO·LONDON·SYDNEY·AUCKLAND

To Austin Diane Jacobson

RL 4, 008-012

IF I DIE BEFORE I WAKE
A Bantam Book / October 1996

Sweet Valley High® and Sweet Valley Twins® are
registered trademarks of Francine Pascal.

Conceived by Francine Pascal.

Produced by Daniel Weiss Associates, Inc.
33 West 17th Street
New York, NY 10011.

Cover art by Sandro Rodorigo.

ISBN: 0-553-48344-7

Published simultaneously in the United States and Canada

Bantam Books are published by Bantam Books, a division of Bantam
Doubleday Dell Publishing Group, Inc. Its trademark, consisting of the
words "Bantam Books" and the portrayal of a rooster, is Registered in the
U.S. Patent and Trademark Office and in other countries. Marca
Registrada. Bantam Books, 1540 Broadway, New York, New York 10036.

PRINTED IN THE UNITED STATES OF AMERICA

OPM   0 9 8 7 6 5 4 3 2 1

One

◇

On the widow's walk of the old Victorian mansion, the creature turns to face her prey. Her lips curl up into an evil smile. At last, she thinks. After all these years she has them just where she wants them.

An icy wind blows across the rooftop. The creature takes a step forward in the chill of the night. Near the edge of the roof the two boys and the three girls huddle against each other. One of the girls is sobbing, her blond hair blowing wildly in the night breeze. A boy has a face as white as a sheet. All look wet. Cold. Forlorn.

A chuckle escapes the creature's throat.

Another step forward. And another. The creature fixes her victims with a victorious stare. She's been waiting for this moment.

"Welcome," she hisses. Thunder crashes violently,

and the railing stands out in a brilliant flash of lightning. "Welcome to your worst nightmare."

She pauses, searching the faces in front of her and relishing the looks of terror she sees.

"And welcome," she adds in the softest of whispers. "Welcome to your death."

Raindrops pelted against Elizabeth Wakefield's face as she stood on the widow's walk. Above her head thunder roared ominously. Elizabeth's twin sister, Jessica, was sobbing with fright. But Elizabeth had eyes only for the monstrous girl in front of her. Wrapped in a ragged nightgown, the figure stepped slowly, deliberately forward.

This can't be happening, Elizabeth thought desperately. *It can't!* She dug her fingernails into her palm so hard, her hand hurt. *It's only a dream,* she told herself. *It isn't real. It can't be.*

But it was.

"Take it away!" Winston Egbert sobbed. His fingers scrabbled at the railing. Elizabeth could see him blinking rapidly, as if hoping he could somehow make the monster disappear.

With a peculiar swaying step the creature moved even closer. Elizabeth shrank back. Her eyes swept across the monster's face—the crooked nose, the dead-looking eyes, the horrifyingly scarred flesh. Elizabeth drew in her breath.

"Should we shout for help?" Amy Sutton burrowed against Elizabeth's shoulder.

"No one would hear us. We're too high." Todd Wilkins glanced quickly over the rail that separated the widow's walk from the edge of the roof. "We're, like, four floors up, and with the wind the way it is—" He broke off as a sudden gust rattled the roof. To Elizabeth, the noise sounded louder than a jet engine.

"And we can't jump for it either," Amy continued brokenly. "We'd—We'd—" She took a deep shuddering breath. "We'd crash on the ground and—"

And die, Elizabeth finished the sentence in her head. With a sudden hissing sound the beast advanced another step. What was left of its eyes glittered sharply, reminding Elizabeth of the cold steel of a knife blade. She could make out the outlines of a child's bunny slipper on one of the creature's feet.

"Then we'll have to—" Todd swallowed hard.

"What?" Hope rose in Amy's eyes.

"We'll have to, you know, fight it," Todd said dully.

Elizabeth turned to her friend in alarm. "Are you kidding?"

Todd didn't meet her eyes. Taking a deep breath, he moved into a karate stance.

"Todd!" Elizabeth protested. Her heart was

hammering in her chest. The monster was incredibly strong. She knew that from experience.

The creature made another hissing noise. She peered at Todd, a challenge glimmering in her half-dead eyes.

Elizabeth seized his sleeve and held tight. She could feel him shuddering.

"I guess—you're right," he muttered, lowering his arms. "But then what do we do?"

The five kids on the roof stood silently as a bolt of lightning shot down out of the sky. In the distance Elizabeth could hear the wail of fire engines. She wished with all her heart that the firefighters were coming to rescue her and her friends. But she knew they weren't.

They couldn't. No one knew they were there.

The creature took another step forward, smiling to reveal awful, broken teeth. The beast was close enough that Elizabeth could have reached out and touched it if she had wanted to. She shrank backward against the railing. The metal pressed sharply into her body, but she barely noticed the pain.

"What are we going to do?" Todd asked again, a note of panic in his voice.

But Elizabeth only shook her head.

She couldn't see any way out. Her heart began to beat furiously. In the darkness she fumbled for Jessica's hand.

If I'm going to die, she thought, choking down a sob, *at least let my sister escape. . . .*

Jessica sagged against Elizabeth, her whole body racked with sobs. The pressure of Elizabeth's hand helped a little, but not much. A terrible fear gripped her heart.

Desperately she tried to figure out a way to escape from the monster. But she couldn't focus. All she could think about was how she and her friends had gotten into this mess. Like a videotape on fast forward, the events flashed past her eyes, one by one.

It had all started so innocently, Jessica remembered. She, Elizabeth, Amy, Todd, and Winston had been hired to baby-sit the five kids in the Riccoli family, who had just moved into this old abandoned mansion.

Angrily Jessica shook her head. Why had they ever agreed to baby-sit the Riccoli kids? Almost from the start things had gone wrong. Night after night the kids would wake up with horrible, realistic dreams. Jessica shuddered. The image of five-year-old Juliana Riccoli flashed into her mind. Jessica could see Juliana sitting up in bed after one of her nightmares, the little girl's cheeks wet with tears, her breath coming in quick gasps as Jessica tried to calm her down.

And what was worse, the nightmares were all

the same. The children all dreamed about a half girl, half monster who tried to push them down the stairs. Or tried to set their room on fire. Or grabbed them by the throat and tried to choke them. The kids described the exact same creature—right down to the one bunny slipper, the ragged teddy bear, and the faded daisy-print nightgown.

At first, Jessica remembered, she and her sister hadn't taken the kids' dreams seriously. "Dreams are just dreams," she had told seven-year-old Gretchen Riccoli. "They're not real." She could hear her own voice now, trying to reassure the anxious little girl. If she'd only known. . . . She sucked in her breath. *Dreams aren't real. Yeah, right.*

There were other strange things too. Jessica thought of the hidden room on the third floor that had once belonged to a little girl named Eva Sullivan. The dusty old room had been sealed off. It seemed as though nothing inside had been disturbed for years.

Jessica remembered a snapshot labeled "Alice and Eva" on a bulletin board in the hidden room. One of the girls in the picture looked just like Jessica's own mother, Alice Wakefield, when she was a twelve-year-old. But whenever the twins tried to talk to their mother about the mansion or the Sullivan family who used to lived there, Mrs.

Wakefield grew agitated and changed the subject. And Jessica's friends' parents never wanted to talk about it either.

Now Jessica saw in her mind the little girl, Eva. Eva, who had lived here years before. Eva, as she was once and as she was now, the horrible monster who stood before her on the widow's walk. Eva, who for some reason Jessica couldn't imagine, had come for revenge against the kids who lived in her house.

And people who went into the house, period, Jessica reminded herself. Because the nightmares soon affected Jessica and the other baby-sitters too. It seemed that every time she closed her eyes in the Riccoli house, the monster appeared. And Eva kept getting angrier and angrier.

Jessica gulped. She saw herself earlier that very evening, her friends gathered around her in the Riccolis' living room. She saw the Riccolis' ugly furniture, their massive grandfather clock, their curving iron staircase. And she saw herself and her friends, one by one, losing their battle against sleep and closing their eyes. They had planned to sleep for only ten minutes at a time, but the alarm had never gone off. And now—

And now they were all up here on the roof, dreaming and yet not dreaming at the same time. They stood high above the ground in the wind and rain of the dark night. Eva Sullivan's un-face grinned evilly at them and her hideous hand was thrust forward, long fingers pointing at Jessica's own neck.

A scream caught in her throat.

This is a nightmare, she assured herself. *I'm dreaming. We're all dreaming. All we have to do is wake up!*

But Jessica knew the truth.

Somehow her dream had come true.

Deep in her chest, Eva Sullivan snarled—a revolting sound that made Elizabeth long to cover her ears. But she couldn't. She gripped the railing with one hand, and Jessica was clutching her other hand so tightly Elizabeth thought she'd never be able to move her fingers again.

The monster lunged toward the baby-sitters. Amy and Winston dived one way, screeching in terror, while Jessica and Todd scrambled in the opposite direction. Elizabeth tried to move too, but her feet wouldn't budge. Dimly she realized that she had lost her grip on her sister's hand. As if in a trance, she pressed her back against the railing, her eyes focused directly on the beast as it approached.

Eva Sullivan—or what had once been Eva Sullivan—let out a triumphant, unearthly scream.

Elizabeth tried desperately to move her body.

Her brain spun with commands. But she could only stare at the monster.

With a terrible gurgle the creature reached out her fingers. Two or three looked almost normal. The rest had grown into horrible twisting shapes that looked more like vulture's claws. The monster hissed. Elizabeth moaned. At the last possible second she ducked her head to one side, hoping that the sharp, ugly talons would miss. . . .

There was a tearing noise.

Elizabeth's shoulder felt chilly. She could see a gaping hole in the fabric of her sweater.

Eva reached forward with her other hand to try again.

Elizabeth tried to yell, but her voice stuck in her throat. Turning quickly, she pushed against the heavy iron rail behind her. There was only one direction to go. And that was up.

"Elizabeth!" Jessica's cries seemed somehow very far away. Balanced precariously half on and half off the rail, Elizabeth didn't dare turn her head to find her sister. There was an ominous swishing sound at her feet. The beast was coming closer!

Elizabeth bit her lip so hard, she tasted blood. Eva's fingers scratched her ankles. She could feel the monster's awful breath against her cheek. Elizabeth summoned all her strength. She scrambled farther up the railing, trying to hoist her body higher than Eva could reach.

"Elizabeth!" Jessica's voice sounded terror stricken.

Too late Elizabeth felt the world fall out from beneath her body. *I'm going over the edge!* she realized in horror. For a split second she balanced on top of the railing that separated the roof of the old mansion from the ground four stories below. She backpedaled furiously, trying to swing her legs onto the safety of the widow's walk. But she knew it was no use. She could feel herself hurtling headfirst over the railing.

And now two screams mixed together in the night air. One was Jessica's and the other, Elizabeth realized, was her own.

"Help!" she cried, even though she knew that she was the only one who could save herself. Frantically she turned in midair and made a grab for the iron rail. It was all that could keep her from tumbling to the ground.

Reach! Elizabeth commanded herself, wishing her arms were ten feet long. She stretched as far as she could go. *I'm not going to make it*, she realized in terror. She could see the top of the iron railing flash past her fingertips, and Elizabeth shut her eyes in despair, hoping that by some miracle, she would somehow survive the crash—

When suddenly something brushed against her elbow.

Elizabeth's reflexes took over. In that tiniest fraction of a second she reached out her hand and grabbed whatever it was tight. *A wrist,* she thought gratefully. That was it, all right. One of her friends had reached down to save her! Her body thudded against the side of the rail, so hard she could feel a bruise rising instantly on her ribs, but she didn't care.

"Pull me up!" she yelled breathlessly, her voice shaking so badly she barely recognized it. "You saved my life!" A weak feeling of relief washed over her as she hung there in the darkness, her fingers firmly clutching the wrist that had saved her from certain death. *Was it Todd?* she wondered, opening her eyes and straining to see. *Or Amy?* Whoever this was had real muscles, that was for sure. It wasn't Winston, anyway—

Elizabeth's blood turned to ice as she saw the arm extending over the iron rail of the widow's walk. A gruesome, horribly twisted arm. A mangled, crooked arm.

The arm of the hideous beast.

Elizabeth tried to shriek, but once again no sound came out. Her mouth felt dry as a bone. She stared up into the inky blackness of the night. Beyond the arm was the grotesque face, the face she knew so well from all the night-mares. Elizabeth's eyes locked with the mon-ster's.

Eva stared back at her. For what seemed like an eternity, Elizabeth swung at the end of the girl's arm, the night sky wobbling above her. All that existed for Elizabeth was herself—and the girl-beast that held her tight.

Slowly, powerfully, Eva began to dig her claw-like fingers into Elizabeth's flesh. Elizabeth winced as the grip grew stronger and tighter. Tears stung her eyes. To be so close to safety and yet so far . . .

"Don't," she pleaded, beginning to sob. "Save me, please, I'll do anything—"

The monster's eyes narrowed. Eva let out a deep, ugly laugh that sounded like the thunder rumbling in the sky overhead.

"Please—" Elizabeth had never felt such pain. She was certain the creature would draw blood any minute. Her hand was drenched in sweat, and she could feel herself beginning to lose her grip on Eva. "Please!" *How do you reason with a nightmare?* she wondered. With her free hand she groped for the railing, the roof, the frame of the house, but she was too far away.

Eva's nails dug in harder. Despite her best efforts, Elizabeth was sliding lower. Desperately she stared up at the beast, pleading with her eyes. She scanned Eva's face, hoping for some sign of sympathy, some expression of pity, of kindness.

But there was none.

"Elizabeth!" Elizabeth could hear Jessica yelling to her from the roof. "Hold on tight!"

"Save yourselves!" Elizabeth tried to shout, loud enough for her sister and the others to hear. Her wrist ached terribly. Blood began to ooze down her forearm. In a few short seconds there would be nothing left to support her. She would tumble straight down, like a meteorite.

And then it all would be over.

At least Jessica and the others might escape.

Sobbing, Elizabeth tore her gaze away from the steely eyes of the beast above her. For the briefest of instants she looked down toward the ground. It was only four stories below, but it looked like four miles. She tried to kick her legs and swing back up over the railing, but it was no use. Her body felt heavy, leaden, exhausted.

Sobbing, Elizabeth shut her eyes.

There was the sound of thunder.

And then her fingers clutched nothing at all, and Elizabeth felt her body plunging down, down, down . . .

Two

That's strange, Elizabeth thought. She'd braced her body for the crash, but it hadn't come.

And now the sky was white for some reason. White and lit up bright as day, when it had just been dark and stormy on the roof. Hadn't it?

Elizabeth could no longer hear Jessica's screams sounding in her ears, but there was a loud sobbing instead. *Maybe it's me*, she thought vaguely. She didn't think Jessica's voice would carry this far down. Unless Eva Sullivan had thrown her sister over the side of the mansion too . . .

Tentatively Elizabeth tried to wiggle her big toe. It moved. In turn she tried moving her little finger, her eyebrow, her neck, her shoulder—*Ouch!* That one hurt plenty, and Elizabeth winced. Her ribs ached too. In fact, her whole body was a little sore.

She frowned. *But shouldn't I be a lot sorer than this if I've just fallen four stories?*

The sobbing seemed louder.

Eva? Even the thought of the creature that had attacked her up on the roof made Elizabeth's heart work double time. Suddenly it became very important to know exactly where she was. Forcing herself to remain calm, Elizabeth took a deep breath and strained to focus her eyes.

The whiteness above her spun crazily. It couldn't possibly be the sky, that was for sure. The sky didn't have a gash in it, did it? And what was that weird bright object off to the side? The sun? *No way*, Elizabeth told herself, blinking hard. She concentrated on getting her eyes to work together. Maybe she was dead. Or dreaming. Could you have a dream within a dream? Or a dream within a dream that was only partly a dream and partly real?

Elizabeth's whole right side felt heavy. Closing one eye, she stared hopefully up at the sky with the other. For a fraction of a second the picture swung crazily back and forth, then just as suddenly resolved into—a ceiling.

A ceiling? Outside on the lawn? Slowly opening the other eye, Elizabeth stared up. *A white plaster ceiling,* she thought, *with a crack on one side, and that bright thing over there, that's a chandelier of course, and—*

A sound interrupted her. *Bong. Bong. Bong.*

All at once Elizabeth knew precisely where she was—the Riccoli living room. The chiming came from the grandfather clock. Five chimes altogether. *Five o'clock in the morning!* She had never been so glad to wake up.

I'm out of the dream! she exulted. *I've escaped!* Feeling as if a thousand-pound weight had been taken off her shoulders, she looked around at the same old ugly furniture, the familiar spiral staircase that led to the second floor, the doors, the halls. She breathed deeply. And suddenly tears began to sting her eyes.

I was so scared, she thought, her whole body trembling at the memory of the dream. *Oh, man, I was so frightened—*

"Libabeff?"

A small voice at her elbow made her start. "What is it?" she said.

"Libabeff? I scared."

Elizabeth looked down. The youngest Riccoli child, two-year-old Nate, nestled in the crook of her right arm. *That was the sobbing noise,* she realized. "Nate!" she said, looking at the little boy. "How did you get out of your crib?"

Nate stared back at Elizabeth. His eyes looked tired. His lower lip trembled.

"Nate scared," he explained, clenching and unclenching his fists. "Nate thinked Libabeff— dead." A big tear spilled out of the corner of one eye. And Nate threw himself across Elizabeth's chest, holding her tightly, his body racked with sobs.

Elizabeth rocked him gently. "It's OK, Nate," she crooned. "I—I thought maybe I was dead too, but I—I guess I'm not." She stroked Nate's forehead, and then she began to cry too.

"Elizabeth?" A sleepy voice from across the room spoke up. "Are you—" The voice caught. "I mean, is that really you?"

Jessica, Elizabeth realized. She had forgotten all about her sister. "Oh, Jess, it's OK," she choked out. "I'm here—and I guess—I guess she's gone."

"Big ugly girl gone?" Nate demanded.

Elizabeth scarcely heard. She glanced around the room. There was Winston, sprawled across the couch, rubbing his eyes and moaning. Nearby, Amy sat curled in a chair, a what's-going-on expression on her face. And Todd was slumped at her feet, yawning and stretching like the lions at the Sweet Valley Zoo when they'd just woken up. *They're all here.* Elizabeth's heart leaped.

And the monster's nowhere in sight.

She hugged little Nate as tightly as she could. She felt totally exhausted, but she didn't care.

We're all safe!

"I guess we all—fell asleep," Jessica said thickly. She hated the sensation of just waking up. Her tongue felt too big for her mouth, her voice sounded dorky, and she couldn't quite get the feeling back into her left hand, and—

And mostly she didn't want to think about what she had just been dreaming.

"I guess so," Todd said tonelessly. He slumped against the couch. "Did anybody else—I mean, did any of you see—" He paused. "You know who?"

It seemed to Jessica as if a little sigh passed through the room. She tensed her muscles. Yes, she most certainly did know who. But no way was she going to say it. Talking about—you know who—would only make her dream seem more vivid, more real.

"I wish we'd never taken this stupid job," she said instead, hoping to steer the subject to something safer.

"That isn't going to help, Jess." Elizabeth shook her head sadly. "We can't get out of this mess by wishing. We have to think about what happened."

Typical Elizabeth, Jessica thought, gritting her teeth. She and her sister looked exactly alike. Each girl had blue-green eyes, long blond hair, and a dimple in her cheek. But inside, the twins were totally different. Jessica lived for parties, fashion, and gossip, while Elizabeth preferred to spend her time with a good book or with one or two close friends. And while Jessica tried to avoid thinking about things that weren't that much fun to think about, Elizabeth was serious and practical.

Why does Elizabeth have to be so sensible all the time? Jessica asked herself. As far as she was concerned, the less they thought about that awful nightmare, the better. She sighed loudly. "I mean, I'm sorry Mrs. Riccoli's mother got sick, in Georgia or wherever—"

"Florida," Winston interrupted. "Mrs. Riccoli had to go see her sick mother in *Florida*."

"Florida, Georgia, who cares?" Jessica snapped. She did her best to shove the image of her dream out of her mind: all five of them on the roof of the building somehow, and rain pelting down, and thunder rattling, and lightning so bright she could see it even with her eyes shut.

And—her. It. Whatever. Jessica shut her eyes firmly, but she could still see every line and feature of Eva's body. She shivered. For all she knew, that picture was permanently etched into her memory, and she'd never sleep again.

"And Mr. Riccoli's in Sacramento, where he's still got his old job," Winston was saying in a singsong kind of voice, "and so we're the only ones who can baby-sit." He looked from Jessica to little Nate, sleeping now in Elizabeth's arms. "And that's why we're here."

"I *knew* that, thank you very much," Jessica said, rolling her eyes. "What I *meant* was . . ." Her voice trailed off. What had she meant? She couldn't remember. "Never mind," she grumbled.

"I hope—" Amy shook her head and huddled closer to Elizabeth. "I hope Mrs. Riccoli comes back soon."

"She should be coming back tomorrow," Todd said. He motioned to the grandfather clock. "I mean, today. You know."

Jessica shook her head as she followed his gaze. *Ten minutes after five in the morning. Great. Just great.* "I am not staying another *second* in this house," she announced. Getting up, she began to pace through the living room. Her hand still ached. "I don't care what Mrs. Riccoli will say, I don't care about the money, I don't care about anything except saving my own life!" Her voice caught, and she realized to her dismay that she was beginning to cry. "I've got to get out of here before *she*—"

Jessica caught herself, but not soon enough. There was an awful silence. Then Elizabeth nodded.

"So," she said slowly. "You dreamed it too."

And Jessica couldn't hold back her tears any longer.

"OK," Elizabeth said softly a few minutes later. Nate was still asleep in her lap, and the other baby-sitters were gathered around her on the couch. She sat up straighter, trying to ignore the pain in her shoulder. "We'll compare notes. Where was your dream? Amy?"

Amy's long straight hair was hopelessly tangled. Elizabeth watched her friend nibble nervously on a strand as she considered the question. "On—" Amy swallowed hard. "On the roof."

Elizabeth bit her lip. Just as she'd thought. "On the roof of this house?" she probed gently.

"Uh-huh." Amy nodded slowly. "Up on the, I don't know what you call it, the flat place with a rail, right in the front of the building?"

"The widow's walk." Todd let out a low whistle. "Mine too."

"Same here." Winston drummed his fingers against the coffee table. Quickly he blew his cheeks out and in—once, twice, three times. "I mean, yeah. Up there. You know. The same place." He took a deep breath and pointed to Amy. "What she said."

Elizabeth could feel her heart beginning to race. "Jessica?" She turned to her sister.

Jessica could only nod.

"All right. Mine was too." Elizabeth took a deep breath. "And the weather?"

"The worst storm in, like, the whole history of the entire world," Winston said before anyone else could speak. "Flashes of lightning so big I thought I'd die. And thunderbolts louder than acid rock music."

"Check," Todd said grimly.

"Lightning," Jessica gasped, shutting her eyes and then opening them right away.

"And thunder." Amy took a deep breath. "Next time there's a thunderstorm, I'll probably hide under the bed with my dog." She laughed nervously, but no one joined in.

Elizabeth moved forward, her ribs sending shivers of pain through the rest of her body. Her heart was beating quickly. "Was there—you know, anybody else on the widow's walk with us?" she asked, dreading the answer.

The other four baby-sitters all looked at the floor. The only sound in the room was the ticking of the grandfather clock. All the lights in the room were on. Still, Elizabeth wished for more light, more noise. *Anything that made it seem more like daytime,* she thought, suppressing a nervous shudder.

When no one spoke, Elizabeth clutched her sister's hand. "OK," she said, her mouth feeling dry. "Just nod yes if what I say matches what you saw. And if it doesn't, say 'No' as loud as you possibly can. All right?"

There were halfhearted nods around the circle.

"OK." Elizabeth took a deep breath. "One bunny slipper," she said, hoping that someone would bellow "No!" right in her ear.

But all she saw were four tiny nods.

"A nightgown. In a flowery print."

Nods again. "Yellow flowers," Amy muttered.

"Daisies," Jessica said, clutching her twin's hand.

Elizabeth hesitated. "A face that—isn't exactly there." She looked from one baby-sitter to another. All around the circle heads were nodding.

"But it can't be," Todd muttered. "It doesn't make sense! She—it—couldn't have been in everybody's dream! There's no possible way!" He rocked forward on his heels. "You guys know what I'm talking about, don't you?" he appealed. "I mean—I guess she could have been in all the dreams, but that's just *dreams*, it isn't *real*, don't you see?" He paused. "Don't you?" he asked in a forlorn voice.

Once again there was utter silence. Elizabeth could feel Nate's chest rising and falling with each little breath he took.

"Don't you?" Todd pleaded.

"We've seen her before," Jessica said, winding a lock of hair around her little finger over and over again. "You have too. You know she's—it's—real."

"Yeah, but—" Todd looked imploringly around the room.

"The monster made a hissing sound when she breathed," Winston said softly. "Hands up if you heard that."

Amy drew in her breath. "That was the scariest part." She lifted her hand, trembling, into the air. Slowly but firmly, Winston raised his own hand. So did Jessica. Elizabeth shut her eyes, remembering without wanting to remember the noises that the creature had made as it lunged toward her on the roof. "I heard hissing too," she half whispered.

Todd blinked rapidly. "But that still doesn't *mean* anything," he argued. "It doesn't, like, *prove* that it was real!" He clenched his fists so hard, his knuckles turned white. "Now if someone had, you know, a scar from the monster or something—"

A scar from the monster. Elizabeth drew in her breath. She suddenly knew why her shoulder ached so much.

Slowly, deliberately, she swiveled her neck to see.

There on her shoulder, beneath the torn ribbons of her sweater, were three angry gashes about two inches long and three quarters of an inch deep.

They looked like the mark of a vulture's claw—

Only sharper. And more twisted.

"Then it *was* real," Jessica said at last. She forced herself to keep calm. "I guess—that's why my hand hurts so much. Remember, Lizzie?" She turned to her sister. "The way you were grabbing my hand out there on the roof? You were crying so hard, I thought you were going to have a heart attack or something."

"*I* was sobbing so hard?" Elizabeth gave Jessica a funny look. "*You* were the one who—"

Jessica sighed loudly. Her sister could be so difficult sometimes. "Well, whatever," she said with a sniff. "Anyway—that's why my hand hurts." She flexed it, wincing.

"And that's why my leg is so sore,"

Winston put in. "Remember how you knocked me over, Amy?"

"Me?" Amy opened her eyes wide.

"Yeah, you," Winston replied. "When Eva came at us, and I cleverly ducked, and you practically ran up my back, trying to get away—"

"That wasn't me!" Amy glared at Winston. "That was *you!*"

Winston dropped his eyes to the floor. "Well, it was one of us, anyway," he muttered to no one in particular.

Amy turned to Elizabeth. "Then you must be pretty beat up," she said in a tone of wonderment. "Eva banged you around a lot. Does anything else hurt?"

Elizabeth nodded. "Well, there's my wrist where she dug her claws in. And my ribs, and my hand—" Gently she rolled up her sleeve, revealing ugly gashes on her wrist.

Jessica gasped and shrank back. The gashes looked uglier than the marks on Elizabeth's shoulder. Not as long, but deeper and somehow—

Angrier. That was the word.

"Ga-ross," Winston muttered, screwing up his eyes.

Amy bit her lip. "We'd better take care of that," she said. "There must be ointment and bandages somewhere."

Jessica felt just a teeny bit jealous of her sister's wounds. Elizabeth was certainly getting a lot of attention. For a brief moment Jessica wished she'd been the one who got pushed off the widow's walk. But as she looked more closely at the wounds, she changed her mind. They really did look ugly.

"I hope the medical supplies aren't upstairs," Elizabeth said, looking up to the dark landing above their heads.

"What's the matter, afraid of a little darkness?" Winston jeered.

"Yeah," Elizabeth admitted. She thrust the sleeping form of Nate Riccoli toward Winston. "But since you're not, Winston, why don't you put this little guy back in bed again?"

Winston leaped back as if Elizabeth had just handed him a bomb. "Are you out of your mind?" he gasped. "Sweet little innocent old me? Go up *there?* Surely you jest."

Jessica let out her breath. "Cut it out, Winston," she snapped.

With a nervous grin Winston looked around from one person to another. "Surely you jest," he repeated. "Come on, guys, laugh! It's funny! You know, ha-ha-ha and tickle my funny bone?"

"Save it, Winston," Todd said tiredly.

And Jessica could only agree. *In broad daylight,*

during science class, that'd be funny, she said to herself.

But not here. Not now.

Right now, she thought with a deep scowl, *nothing could possibly be funny.*

Nothing in the entire world.

Three

This is the longest night in history, Jessica thought numbly, watching the hands of the grandfather clock creep toward six. It had taken at least three years to get even that far. She watched the second hand crawl forward. A snail could move faster than that, she thought.

Beside her Winston stirred. "Is it light outside?" he whispered.

Todd moved the curtains and stared out the window. "Not yet," he replied gloomily.

Jessica lifted her eyes from the clock and counted to ten as slowly as she could. Glancing back at the clock, she saw to her dismay that only four seconds had passed. *What was that word on the last vocabulary test that meant "endless"?* she wondered. Normally she didn't like to think about school. But now she needed something boring to focus on. E *something*. E—e—

Eternal, that was it. This was an eternal night.

"Maybe we should sing or something," Elizabeth suggested doubtfully. "Row, row, row your boat—stuff like that?"

Jessica's only answer was a snort.

"Well, we've got to stay awake!" Elizabeth insisted. "Remember what happened last time we went to sleep?"

"Don't remind me," Amy said.

"Probably the sun will never rise again," Winston said dolefully. "Probably the world will stay dark forever. No one will ever wake up again, and eventually we'll have to fall asleep ourselves, and then Eva Sullivan will torment us for the rest of our lives." He thought for a moment. "Which won't be much longer, come to think of it."

Jessica didn't know which was worse—Elizabeth's stupid juvenile ideas or Winston's gloominess. She stole a quick glance back at the clock. Less than a minute had passed since the last time she'd looked. She could have sworn it had been half an hour.

"Yeah, come on, guys." Amy's voice was unsteady. "We've got to stay awake somehow. Any ideas?"

"The Weather Channel?" Todd asked doubt-fully.

Jessica yawned. "Yeah, right," she said ungra-ciously. "That would *put* us to sleep."

"Then you think of something better!" Todd glared at her.

"In your dreams," Jessica muttered, then de-cided that was exactly the wrong thing to say. She scrunched deeper into the couch. The trouble was, they were right. Anything was better than falling asleep in this house.

And I guess no one ever died from singing "Row, Row, Row Your Boat."

"All right," she grumbled at last. "One. Two. One, two, three, four. Row, row, row your boat—"

"One for my master, and one for my dame," Elizabeth sang wearily. How long had they been singing? she wondered. Forty-five minutes? An hour? Two years? "And one for—"

Wait a minute.

Her friends had stopped singing along. Instead they were staring at the curtains that cov-ered the window behind her.

Todd drew in his breath and pulled back the curtain. "Look, guys."

In the distance Elizabeth could hear the chat-tering of birds and the comforting noise of a de-livery truck. But what she noticed most was a faint light just beginning to shoot up into the dark sky.

"The sun," Elizabeth said. So far only the tiniest sliver was peeking above the horizon, but even that little glow made Elizabeth feel warm all over. Without knowing quite why, she felt her eyes fill with tears.

"I thought I'd never see it again," Amy murmured.

"*You* thought you'd never see it again?" Winston crowed. "I was so sure *I'd* never see it again, I promised I'd never crack another joke in my whole life—if the sun would only rise."

"And you're planning to keep that promise, I hope?" Todd managed a half smile.

"Um—" Winston looked at his feet and wiggled his toes. "Yeah, well, you know." He shrugged. "I have, like, this really short memory, OK?"

"As *if*," Todd shot back with a grin.

By now Elizabeth could see nearly half the sun, its rays casting a pinkish glow across the whole sky. She sighed again with relief, glad that she had survived the night. Glad that her friends were all in one piece. Glad that Eva Sullivan was gone, at least for now. Glad to see the sun rising slowly but steadily and brightening the entire world.

"The famous poet Winston von Egbert will now recite from his work 'The Glorious Sun,'" Winston said, taking a ridiculous pose by the coffee table. "The sun! The sun!" he declaimed loudly. "My kingdom for a honey bun!"

Elizabeth couldn't help giggling.

"That's the chorus," Winston explained. "You can join in if you want." He cleared his throat. "They sat awake all night," he went on dramatically. "Except for two hours."

"More like a year," Jessica muttered, suppressing a smile.

"No interruptions from the peanut gallery," Winston said frostily. "Might I continue?" He didn't wait for an answer but went on: "They drank lots of coffee. And, um—" He thought hard. "And ran around on towers."

Amy groaned but also laughed.

"Now the chorus," Winston reminded them. Swinging his arms like an orchestra conductor, he chanted: "The sun! The sun!"

"My kingdom for a honey bun!" the others chanted back.

Elizabeth took a deep breath and watched the sun grow in size and intensity. *We did it*, she thought. *The danger's over, for now, anyway, and everybody's all right.*

And under the circumstances even Winston's stupid poems sounded pretty good!

*   *   *

"Would you pour me some cereal, Jessica, please?" Juliana Riccoli asked politely.

Jessica grinned. "Sure, Juliana," she said. "And while I'm at it, would you scoop me some orange juice?"

Juliana looked bewildered. "Huh?" she said.

Jessica patted the five-year-old on the head. "Joke," she said. "Never mind."

It was nine in the morning, and Jessica felt as if she was running on empty. Todd, Amy, and Winston had gone home to get some sleep, leaving the twins alone in the house with the five Riccoli children. By now four of the kids were awake. Nate, Juliana, seven-year-old Gretchen, and eight-year-old Andrew were sitting around the breakfast table. Only the oldest, ten-year-old Olivia, was still asleep.

The kids look pretty well rested, Jessica thought, her gaze traveling around the table. *I wish I did too!*

Andrew slammed his glass of milk down on the table. "Hey, Jessica!" he said loudly. "Can we watch TV this morning after breakfast? Can we? Huh? Huh? Huh?"

"Yeah, please?" Gretchen chimed in. "Pleeeease?"

"Fee Bee! Fee Bee!" Nate chanted. "Want watch Fee Bee!"

Jessica exchanged glances with her sister, who

nodded. "I think you probably could," Jessica said. After all, she reasoned, it would keep the kids out of their hair for a while. She and Elizabeth could certainly use a rest.

"First we watch *Dancing Pink Elephants*," Gretchen said. "Then we can—"

"No way!" Andrew glared at her, milk dribbling from the corners of his mouth. *He looks like my brother, Steven, when he does that,* Jessica thought, disgusted. A picture of her fourteen-year-old know-it-all brother at breakfast popped into her mind. "We're gonna watch *Dracu-Killer,* that's what we're gonna watch!"

"Don't be silly," Gretchen said in her most mature voice. "*Dracu-Killer* is a *dumb* show. I mean, like, *really* dumb. And it's too scary for Nate, anyway."

"Uh-uh!" Andrew rubbed Nate on the back. "Nate *loves Dracu-Killer,* don't you, kiddo?"

"*Ackoo-Kiwer!*" Nate shouted. He gave his cup an imitation karate blow. It tumbled off his high chair tray and onto the ground. Jessica sighed. "Stuck you bwood!"

"*Suck your blood,* you mean," Andrew said with a grin. "See, Nate wants to watch my show."

"In your dreams," Gretchen said. She leaned down to Nate. "Say, 'I want to watch *Dancing Pink Elephants,*' OK? Say '*Dancing Elephants.*'"

"*Danning Ephants*," Nate said agreeably. He pushed his muffin onto the floor. "Want watch *Danning Ephants*." Raising his arms like a ballerina, he grinned proudly.

Jessica laughed. Slowly she brought a glass of milk to her lips.

"Let's let Nate decide," Elizabeth suggested, her eyes twinkling.

"Oh, good grief." Andrew curled his lip at his little brother. "Say *Dracu-Killer* and I'll give you a cookie," he cajoled.

"Say *Dancing Pink Elephants* and I'll give you *two* cookies," Gretchen chimed in.

Nate considered carefully. Then he grinned broadly. "*Danning Ackoo-Kiwer Ephants!*" he shouted.

Jessica choked on her milk just as the phone rang. "I'll get it!" she called out, grabbing the receiver. "Hello," she said. Then, remembering she wasn't at home, she added: "Riccoli house."

"Hello, there!" A familiar warm voice was at the other end of the line. "This is Mrs. Riccoli. I'm sorry, I don't know whether this is Elizabeth or Jessica?"

Jessica grinned. Few people could tell them apart, even over the phone. "Jessica," she said.

"Jessica," Mrs. Riccoli repeated. "Well, I'm here at the airport. My mom is OK, thank goodness, and she's going to be OK—so I'll be home as soon as I can get through the traffic."

Jessica's heart leaped. "Oh, that's great news!"

"Great news that my mom's OK or that I'm back home again?" Mrs. Riccoli asked teasingly.

Jessica turned red. "Well—both," she admitted.

"Everything went all right, I hope?" Mrs. Riccoli asked. Without waiting for an answer, she plunged on. "Well, of course everything was fine, with baby-sitters like you and your sister. I don't know how to thank you. I can't imagine what I would have done if you hadn't agreed to watch the kids."

"Oh." Jessica decided not to mention how deeply she'd been wishing they *hadn't* agreed.

"Of course, I know you couldn't exactly have said no," Mrs. Riccoli went on. "But when I called you in a panic and said my plane was leaving in half an hour and could you baby-sit— well, I just knew that you and your sister would come through!"

Jessica cleared her throat. No, they couldn't exactly have said no—and she couldn't exactly tell Mrs. Riccoli about some half girl, half monster who haunted them in their dreams. Mrs. Riccoli would think they were nuts. "Um, would you like to say hello to the kids?" she asked.

"No, thanks," Mrs. Riccoli said breezily. "I'll be seeing them soon enough. Feel free to park them in front of the TV. I'll be home in an hour or so. And thanks again." There was a click. Mrs. Riccoli had hung up.

One hour. Breathing a sigh of relief, Jessica looked at the phone in her hand.

One more hour in this house.

And then she would never set foot in it again.

"All right." Elizabeth scanned the television listings and suppressed a yawn. Boy, was she ever tired. "Looks like you're all in luck. *Dancing Pink Elephants* is on starting right now, and *Dracu-Killer* is on next."

"All *right!*" Gretchen clapped and nudged Juliana. "Let's go!" The kids scampered into the living room. Olivia, all dressed, hurried down the steps to join them. Elizabeth could hear the television being turned on.

"Yes, it's the Amazing Six-in-One Vegetable Peeler!" a voice bellowed from the screen. "It peels anything you like! Turn it this way and slice up cucumbers, apples, and potatoes! Turn the knife blade up to 'high' and watch the skin come off those hard-to-peel squashes and eggplants! Turn it to 'extra high' and buzz the rind right off your watermelons!"

"Turn the volume down to extra low!"

Elizabeth cried out, catching her sister's eye. Together they walked into the living room and plopped down side by side on the big couch. On the TV screen a man was demonstrating how to set the knife blade so the Amazing Six-in-One Vegetable Peeler would skin a coconut.

Jessica sighed. "I don't know about you," she said, curling up against a pillow. "But I'm *beat*."

"It was a long night, that's for sure," Elizabeth agreed. "Still, it's all over, and we're going home soon." She settled back onto the soft cushions. Then she yawned.

Jessica yawned too.

Elizabeth was so tired, she could barely move her lips into a grin. "Careful!" she warned her sister, yawning again. "It's—um—catching."

"I—" Jessica yawned and shut her eyes. "I know."

"We really—shouldn't—" Elizabeth began. Her own eyelids were feeling heavy. For a fraction of a second she let them close. It felt so good. Opening them again was hard. She yawned once more. "Shouldn't—"

"Shouldn't fall—asleep," Jessica finished, sinking lower into the couch. "You never know what—might—get in our dreams."

"So we won't." Elizabeth found her eyes had drifted shut again. She forced them open. On the TV screen the commercial had ended and the theme song for *Dancing Pink Elephants* had begun. Five incredibly thin pink elephants in tutus paraded through a jungle, singing, "We are the Dancing Elephants! We dance everywhere we can. . . ."

"They don't always dance," Juliana complained. "Sometimes they walk."

"Shhh," Andrew whispered crossly. "I can't hear."

Elizabeth smiled weakly. Afraid she would fall asleep that very minute, she forced herself to focus on the elephants' song.

"We always sing in chorus," the elephants sang. "And we help our fellow man."

"They mean elephants," Juliana said doubtfully. "Don't they mean their fellow elephants, Gretchen?"

Don't fall asleep, Elizabeth ordered herself. She thought she could count on Jessica to stay awake, no matter what, but she was too tired to turn and see how her sister was doing. *Don't fall asleep.* "Hey, um, kids?" she asked drowsily.

"Yeah?" Andrew asked, not taking his eyes off the screen.

Elizabeth's eyes snapped suddenly shut. Her body ached all over. "Um—don't let us fall asleep, OK?" she asked.

"Sure," Andrew said carelessly. "Hey, this is a rerun. It's the one where they dance into the river to save the mean rattlesnake from drowning and it becomes their friend, right?"

"Hey, yeah," Olivia said, crowding closer.

Elizabeth yawned more deeply than ever. "Don't forget, now . . ." she said, but she wasn't sure if anyone could hear her. *It doesn't matter, anyway,* she consoled herself.

Because there's no way I'm going to—
Going to—fall—

Four

Jessica sat up and yawned. *What was that noise?*

"I'll get you, Dracu-Killer!" a voice boomed out.

"Never! Ha, ha, ha!" answered a higher, shriller voice.

Oomph! It sounded as though someone had just kicked someone else in the side.

"Ow!"

Oomph! Oomph!

"Ow!"

Jessica's eyes flickered open in alarm. What in the world was going on?

The second voice spoke again. "I will suck your blood!"

"No way!" The first voice was contemptuous. "I represent the law, Dracu-Killer, and your evil deeds have come to an end!"

Dracu-Killer. Suddenly the name registered in Jessica's mind. But how could *Dracu-Killer* be on? That show about the elephants had begun just a second ago.

"Oh, I love this part!" Gretchen announced, staring eagerly at the screen. "This is where the cops get Dracu-Killer and put him in jail so he can bust out again for the next episode."

Jessica stared in horror at the screen. The police officer was slapping a pair of handcuffs on the funny-looking vampire. *This was the second show the kids were planning to watch*, she thought. *And it's almost over.*

Which could mean only one thing—she had been asleep for nearly an hour.

She looked at the still form of her sister beside her. No doubt about it. Elizabeth was sound asleep.

"I don't believe this!" Jessica groaned. Frantically she pinched, pulled, and pushed Elizabeth. "Lizzie, wake up!" she demanded.

Elizabeth stirred. "Huh?" she murmured.

She's all right, Jessica thought with relief.

"Tune in next week for another exciting episode of—" The TV announcer stopped for a dramatic pause.

"*Ackoo-Kiwer!*" Nate shouted jubilantly.

"*Dracu-Killer!*" the announcer intoned. The picture zoomed in on Dracu-Killer marching off to jail but giving the audience a wink and a thumbs-up signal.

"OK, everybody, that's it," Jessica said, jumping up from her seat. She seized the remote and clicked the on/off button. In an instant the screen went blank.

"Huh?" Elizabeth sleepily rolled over and opened one eye.

"Hey!" Andrew turned and gave Jessica a reproachful look. "I wanted to see the next commercial."

Jessica's heart was beating so hard, she thought it would bounce right out of her body. "Never mind that," she said, her throat almost too dry to talk. "Right now, into the kitchen! You have to clean up after breakfast." She still couldn't believe she had fallen asleep. *I should have known better!* she thought. *I should have known better! I should have—*

A key turned in the lock. Jessica jumped. "Who's there?" she cried, a note of panic in her voice. The picture of a half-girl, half-monster leaped into her mind.

"It's me!" Mrs. Riccoli hurried through the doorway. She stopped short when she saw Jessica. "What's the matter, honey? You look like you've seen a ghost!"

"I guess—I guess I didn't," Jessica managed to stammer out. She felt giddy with relief. She took a couple of tentative steps toward Mrs. Riccoli. "I'm just—glad to see you, is all," she said, breathing deeply.

Boy, am I ever!

"I still can't believe we let ourselves fall asleep while the TV was on," Jessica said glumly, kicking a smooth white pebble down the sidewalk. The twins were walking home from the Riccoli house that morning, their pockets bulging with cash.

"Neither can I." Elizabeth knew she'd been awfully lucky to escape from Eva. She still felt angry at herself for having let her guard down twice in one day. She gave the pebble another kick and watched it scuttle toward a grassy lawn on their right. Maybe they could keep kicking it till they were home. Then she'd keep it as a lucky pebble. "But you know, I think this time was— different, somehow."

"Different?" Jessica frowned at Elizabeth. "Like, how?"

"Well—" Elizabeth wondered how to put it. With the heel of her shoe she dug the pebble out from the edge of the grass and kicked it down to the intersection ahead of them. "Did you have any dreams when we were on the couch?" she asked.

Jessica bit her lip. "Um—I—" Taking a deep

breath, she turned to face her sister. "I guess—I don't know."

"And if you don't know—" Elizabeth prompted her.

"If I don't know," Jessica said slowly, "then—I must not have dreamed about Eva."

"You'd remember if you had," Elizabeth added. She could feel her flesh begin to creep at the thought of Eva. With a shudder she turned to keep walking. "Neither did I. In fact, I had a pretty peaceful sleep."

"It *was* kind of a good sleep, now that you mention it," Jessica admitted. Swinging her foot hard, she kicked the pebble most of the way across the street.

"And we slept for almost exactly an hour," Elizabeth continued. "Two cartoon shows." She stepped off the curb. "That's a lot longer than we were asleep before." She winced. Her shoulder and ribs still hurt.

Jessica sucked thoughtfully on her lip. "Yeah."

"Was there any sign of Eva at all?" Elizabeth asked. "I mean, when you were just waking up or dropping off to sleep?"

Jessica considered. "No," she said at last.

Elizabeth's pulse quickened. "Same here." She smiled shyly at her sister, letting the smile speak the words she couldn't find. *Maybe,* a small voice in her head was saying. *Just maybe.*

Maybe the spell is broken and the monster's gone.

Jessica turned to look at her, eyes full of hope. "Do you think that—" She broke off, biting her lip.

"Could be," Elizabeth murmured wistfully.

On her way up the opposite curb Elizabeth gave the pebble another kick. It bounced crazily off the curb, barely missing the sewer grating. Then it rolled back into the road.

"That was a narrow escape," Elizabeth muttered. Maybe it was a lucky pebble after all.

"What?" Jessica fixed Elizabeth with a look.

"Oh—nothing." Stooping down, Elizabeth grabbed the pebble and stuffed it into her pocket.

A narrow escape, she repeated to herself. Maybe they *had* escaped. Eva hadn't come while they were sleeping on the couch. That was a good sign, all right. Elizabeth rubbed her fingers against her new lucky pebble as they headed down the last block toward home.

"Anything frightening at the haunted mansion yesterday?"

Steven smirked at the twins the next morning. "Down by the ol' scary house," he sang off-key, "my sisters are afraid of every single mouse. Yuk, yuk!"

"Very funny, Steven," Jessica grumbled, reaching for an orange.

"It rhymes, doesn't it?" Steven chugged down a glass of milk in one swallow. Jessica watched in fascination as milk dripped out of the corners of his mouth.

"You know, you look just like Andrew Riccoli when you do that," she commented.

Steven swallowed noisily. "Say what?"

"An eight-year-old," Elizabeth hastened to add. "You look like an eight-year-old we know."

"Oh, Andrew," Steven said. "I know Andrew. Saved his life a couple of weeks ago. Don't tell me you've already forgotten my heroics?" He scratched his fingernails against his chest and blew on them importantly.

Elizabeth rolled her eyes. It was true that Steven had saved Andrew's life after Eva had set his mattress on fire. But in her opinion he was acting just a little too pleased with himself.

"Pardon me while I throw up," Jessica said, pointing to her mouth and pretending to gag.

"Well, I'm glad to hear Andrew's starting to imitate me," Steven remarked. "Kind of figures he'd want a hero like me as a role model, doesn't it?"

Jessica snorted. "Oh, give me a break!"

"Reminds me of a song, in fact," Steven said. His eyes glittered and he let fly a loud burp.

"Oh, that's appealing," Elizabeth remarked, cringing.

Steven picked up a banana and pretended to strum it as if it were a guitar. "Gives you faith that when I'm gone," he sang, "there'll be others left to carry on."

Jessica plugged her ears. The twins had spent most of the previous day asleep, catching up on what they'd missed the night before. One advantage to spending the day in bed, she realized now, was that she hadn't seen much of her brother.

"A guy like me who ain't just a rumor," Steven warbled on, adjusting an imaginary cowboy hat. "A guy who's got my sense of humor. Humor and rumor, get it?" He gave Jessica a thumbs-up sign. "Pretty cool rhyme, huh?"

"Some sense of humor," Jessica grumbled. "Andrew doesn't have your sense of humor, anyway. His is much more sophisticated."

Steven's eyebrows shot up. "A guy my sister thinks is cool. Though he's, like, three grades behind her in elementary school!" He played a final chord on the banana and made kissing noises. "Didn't know you were interested in a *younger* man, darling sister of mine."

"Listen, Andrew Riccoli is just a kid—" Jessica began, putting her hands on her hips and staring daggers at Steven. She could cheerfully have killed her brother. Luckily at that very moment the telephone rang. "I'll get it!" she called out.

"Bet that's lover boy right now," Steven remarked.

It was all Jessica could do not to throw the phone at his head. "Hello?" she said a little too loudly, picking up the receiver.

"Hi." The voice was vaguely familiar. "Um—this is Andrew? Andrew Riccoli?"

"It *is?*" Jessica couldn't stop herself. "I mean, hi. How are you? This is Jessica."

"Oh." Andrew paused. "Um—I just—" He paused again.

"Go on," Jessica encouraged him, not quite daring to call him by name. She glanced at Steven, who was eyeing her with amusement. Quickly she turned her back on him. "What's up, kiddo?"

"Well—none of us had any nightmares last night," Andrew said quickly, the words all running into each other.

"Really? That's great!" Jessica felt a huge sense of relief wash over her. *The nightmare is finally over,* she told herself. She wondered how long had it been since someone had spent a night in that house without having bad dreams. *Maybe not since Eva Sullivan was living there,* she thought.

"And there's other stuff too," Andrew continued. "Daddy is coming for Halloween. And Grandma's OK, and—and—" Andrew groped for words. In the distance Jessica could hear someone talking to him. *Olivia,* she decided. "And nobody had any nightmares. Did I tell you that already?"

"Yes, you did," Jessica said, trying not to laugh. "I'm really happy." *And you could never imagine just how happy I am,* she thought, her eyes shining. "Was that all?"

"Yeah. See you later. Bye." Andrew hung up quickly.

"Who was that?" Elizabeth looked at Jessica curiously as she came back into the dining room.

"Um—one of the Riccoli kids," Jessica answered hastily, not looking at Steven. "It's really good news, Lizzie. None of them had a nightmare last night!"

"Whoopee," Steven said, circling his forefinger in the air.

Elizabeth's eyes lit up. "Great!" she said. "Hey—let's go to Casey's and have a sundae to celebrate!"

"Is it open this early?" Jessica asked in surprise.

Elizabeth shrugged. "Well, if it isn't, we'll camp out by the front door. Just think—we'll never have to worry about Eva Sullivan again!"

Jessica drew in a deep breath. For the first time in what seemed like weeks, she felt completely at peace. *We'll never have to worry about Eva again,* she repeated in her mind. *Never again.*

"You're on!" Jessica pumped her fist into the air. Suddenly she felt energized. "Meet you out front in five minutes!" She dumped the rest of her cereal into the sink and headed for the stairs.

"If I could ask a question?" Steven's voice boomed across the kitchen.

"What?" Jessica asked crossly, stopping at the foot of the steps, anyway.

"You said, *'one* of the Riccolis,'" Steven went on, tugging at his chin. "And what I want to know is, *which* one of the Riccolis? Was it you know who? Huh?" He leaned forward, blinking rapidly.

Whoever invented brothers should have been shot, Jessica thought. She looked at her brother coldly.

"Oh, it was Juliana," she said with a shrug, and headed up the stairs.

Elizabeth's eyes sparkled as she finished the last bit of her sundae. She loved Casey's—the clean marble counter, the old ceiling fan, the rag-time music, and, of course, the ice cream.

And it didn't hurt that Casey's opened at ten o'clock every morning.

"Just over a week till Halloween, you know," she reminded Jessica. With all the scary events of the last few weeks, it had been hard to remember what fun Halloween could be. *I mean*, Elizabeth reminded herself, *who needs pretend tricks and treats when you have your very own monster invading your dreams?*

She laughed. Somehow Eva Sullivan and the old Riccoli mansion seemed very far away. Licking her spoon, she smiled across the table at her sister. "So what are you going to be?"

Jessica dug down into her remaining hot fudge. "*I* am going trick-or-treating as the greatest actress who ever lived," she said proudly.

"You mean Eileen Thomas?" Elizabeth asked, surprised. Eileen Thomas had starred in some movies that Mr. Bowman, their English teacher, had recommended—British films like *Report from a Burning Bridge* and *A Time for Healing*. And Elizabeth's all-time favorite, *Road to Rangoon*. Elizabeth thought Eileen Thomas was wonderful. But she couldn't see Jessica dressing up as—

"Not Eileen Thomas, doofus," Jessica said, rolling her eyes. "Marilyn Monroe, of course!"

Marilyn Monroe—of course! Elizabeth couldn't help smiling. "Not exactly my idea of the world's greatest actress," she said to tease her sister.

"Just goes to show how much *you* know." Jessica shook her head. "So who are you going as?"

Elizabeth's eyes lit up. "Jane Austen," she said.

"Jane *who?*" Jessica demanded.

Elizabeth waved her hand in the air. "No one

you'd know," she said with a grin. "Just one of
the best writers in the English language, that's
all."

"Oh, yeah," Jessica said slowly. "I've heard of
her. Didn't she write, like, two million years ago
or something?"

"Only two *hundred* years ago," Elizabeth said,
leaning forward eagerly. "And her characters are
so interesting and so realistic, they could practically be around today."

"If they could be around today, then what's
the point?" Jessica asked with a shrug. "Was she
friends with—you know, Charles Whozis? The
guy who wrote *Great Expectations*?"

"Dickens," Elizabeth supplied automatically.
They'd read Dickens's novel *Great Expectations* in
school, and she'd loved it almost as much as Jane
Austen's books. "No. She was dead by the time
Dickens came along."

"Bummer," Jessica said carelessly. "I thought
Miss Havisham in *Great Expectations* was kind of
neat. The way she never got over being stood up
by her husband on her wedding day." Her eyes
gleamed. "For the rest of her life all she wanted
was *revenge!* Did Jane Boston write anything
good like that?"

"*Austen.* And she wrote lots of good stuff,"
Elizabeth said, trying to think if any of Austen's
characters spent their lives getting revenge on

someone. "She wrote *Pride and Prejudice*," Elizabeth recited, ticking it off on her index finger. "And, um, *Sense and Sensibility*."

"Oh, I get it!" Jessica said in a singsong voice. "Did she also write *Dweebs and Dorkiness*? Or *Stupidity and*, um, *Steven*?"

Elizabeth chuckled. She and Jessica were so different, they often had trouble seeing eye to eye. But they did agree on one thing: their brother was a total loser! "*Stupidity and Steven*," she said, liking the idea. "Tell you what, *Marilyn*. I'll write that book if you'll star in the film version."

Jessica's face opened up into a huge grin. "It's a deal!" she said with feeling.

Five

◇

"Wall-to-wall people." Elizabeth groaned, looking with dismay through the doors of Sweet
Valley Spooks & More, the costume store at the
mall.

"Well, what did you expect four days before
Halloween?" Jessica asked, surging through the
crowd and into the store. The twins were costume shopping. A full week had passed since
their last nightmare. As far as Jessica was concerned, Eva Sullivan was gone for good.

"Hey, wait up!" Elizabeth's voice already
seemed distant.

Jessica stopped next to a little boy trying on a
vampire outfit six sizes too big and waited for
her sister to catch up. "I don't know why you
don't like crowds," she grumbled good-naturedly.

She took a quick look around at the bustling store. There was nothing she liked better than being in a big group of people—the bigger, the better.

Together the twins edged across the room. People filled every available inch of floor space, pawing through the racks and trying on costumes. Cat costumes. Mummy costumes. Clown, cow, and basketball-player costumes. To her left Jessica could see three fairy princesses. To her right was a guy dressed like a police officer—

Wait a minute. Jessica rubbed her eyes. "No, I take it back," she murmured. "He really *is* a police officer!"

"So what do you think of this one?" a voice asked. Jessica snapped her head up. In front of her was one of the most gorgeous guys she'd ever seen, trying on a vampire costume that looked just like a fancy tuxedo.

"Try the red bow tie," another voice replied. "And if you comb your hair a little more to the right—"

The crowd swept Jessica along too fast for her to hear the rest.

Whistling carelessly, Steven Wakefield scanned the racks of the costume shop, looking for the most grotesque, hideous Halloween outfit he could find.

Yup, Halloween was going to be fun, all right.

His best friend, Joe Howell, nudged him. "How about this?" he asked, motioning toward the wall.

Steven moved back to let a small child in a Dracu-Killer costume through. Then he followed Joe's gaze. Before him hung a lifelike rubber mask, lips twisted into a tortured expression, ugly-looking scars dotting the cheeks. Horribly glowing red lines radiated from a third eye in the center of the forehead. The mask was the ugliest color Steven had ever seen, a sickening cross between green, yellow, gray, and brown.

Steven examined it closely. "Not nearly disgusting enough," he said at last.

Joe nodded knowingly. "That's what I thought too."

Their eyes darted along the endless rows of costumes. In the background a child wailed, "But I *waaaant* it. I *neeeed* it. *Pleeeease?*"

"How about this one?" Joe pointed to a misshapen head with a swollen red tongue protruding through cracked lips. Steven reached out to touch the mask. The fringe of hair, he saw, was really fake spiders. Fiberglass eyeballs rolled back into the head when the mask jiggled.

Steven sighed. "I don't know," he said, wrinkling his nose. "Pretty lame, if you ask me. In fact—" He stepped back, narrowly missing a man leading a couple of dancing pink elephants toward the counter. "This whole place is pretty lame. We're going to have to come up with our own design, I guess."

"Hmmm." Joe shook his head. Steven could see he was still interested in the swollen-tongue mask. "Like, what did you have in mind, man?"

Steven shrugged and jammed his hands deeper into his pockets. "I don't know," he admitted. "But there's got to be something better than *this*." He grimaced, indicating what he thought of Sweet Valley Spooks & More. "Come on," he urged Joe. "Let's go back to my place and—"

He stopped. In the middle of the hubbub he could hear an eerily familiar voice.

"Excuse me, but where are your Marilyn Monroe costumes?"

Jessica, he thought, his lips spreading into a smile. His mind flashed back to the conversations they'd had over the last few weeks about the monster at the Riccoli house.

"Hello?" Joe waved his hand in front of Steven's face. "Earth to Wakefield! Anybody home?"

Steven tried to remember the creature the girls had described. Too bad he hadn't listened carefully. Or maybe the twins had been mumbling. Figured. They just didn't know how to speak clearly.

"Wakefield!" Joe shook him violently by his shoulder. "What's the deal?"

"One slipper," Steven whispered, half to himself. "A nightgown with some kind of flowers on it." That could be embarrassing, but he'd manage it somehow. *Something about a stuffed animal— that'd be easy.* And then the body. How had his sisters described the body?

A face that, like, isn't there.

A twisted leg, with a misshapen foot on the end.

Eyes that look at you as if they're dead. Scars so deep you can almost see down to the bone. Fingernails like demented claws.

"A limp," Steven said out loud. He licked his lips in anticipation. "And a hissing sound when it walked."

Perfect!

"Wakefield! You dead or what?"

Steven gasped. Joe was holding Steven's neck with one hand and waving a fist in front of his eyes with the other. "What's going on, huh?"

Steven grinned, even though having Joe's hand around his neck felt a little uncomfortable. "I know what we're going to be for Halloween," he announced.

"Huh?" Slowly Joe let his fist drop. "What?"

Steven smiled wolfishly. "We're going to go as my sisters' worst nightmare," he said with an evil-sounding chuckle.

*   *   *

Elizabeth frowned. She should have guessed there wouldn't be any Jane Austen costumes in the store. She picked up a brown-checked dress with ruffles on the sleeves and a white lace collar. *Hmmm.* It looked kind of colonial, but maybe it would do.

"But Mo-om!" came a voice from the other side of the rack. "You promised!"

Elizabeth shook her head, remembering when she and Jessica were younger and had waged Halloween battles like that with their own mother. *No,* she corrected herself. *With Dad. Mom never took us Halloween shopping. She never much liked Halloween.*

With a sigh she turned back to the dress. Maybe if she put her hair back and bought a pair of those old granny glasses from the counter rack and carried a quill pen—

"Any luck with Jane Houston?" Jessica swept through the crowd, two boxes held high above her head. "You'll never believe what I got, Lizzie!" she crowed, not waiting for an answer.

"Two costumes?" Elizabeth asked pointedly. "Planning to go trick-or-treating twice or something?"

"Hey, that's a pretty decent idea!" Jessica said. "Maybe I can go Halloween night and then again the next day—"

Elizabeth giggled. "I was just joking, Jess. So what did you find?"

Jessica swung the boxes down between the racks. "You'll *love* them," she declared. "Feast your eyes!"

Elizabeth leaned forward and stared at the topmost box. Inside was a perfect replica of Marilyn Monroe. Dress, mask, hair—the costume looked totally realistic. It was like looking at a photograph of the real actress. "That *is* great, Jessica," she commented, thankful that she wasn't going to wear it herself. "What's in the other one?"

Jessica's eyes shone. "Just wait," she told her sister, bending down and opening the other box. With a magician's flourish she stepped back. "Ta-da!"

Elizabeth drew in her breath. "This one's a beauty," she said. And she meant it too. It was a movie star costume, the colors vibrant, the material smooth and silky. Elizabeth longed to stroke it between her fingers. The diamond tiara looked genuine. "Oh, Jessica, it's great, but—"

"I know, I know," Jessica broke in. "It only comes in adult sizes. I tried on the smallest they had, and even that was too big." She jabbed her finger at the costume. "But it's to die for, don't you think?"

"Yeah, it is," Elizabeth agreed slowly. She was sorry they didn't make the costume in smaller sizes too. She would have gladly gone trick-or-treating in it herself. The ball gown shimmered brightly, even in the harsh light of the store. Elizabeth took a deep breath. "But if it doesn't fit you, then—"

"Ah." Jessica grinned. "See, here's my idea. We're going to get it for Mom."

"For Mom?" Elizabeth frowned. "But Mom never dresses up on Halloween."

"Details, details," Jessica said, waving her hand in the air. "That's because she's never had this costume before. What do you think, she wants to get dressed up like some silly cartoon character?" She pretended to gag.

Elizabeth bit her lip. What Jessica said made some sense. It was true that most costumes weren't her mother's kind of thing. Still, as far back as she could remember, Mrs. Wakefield had hated Halloween. *Mom never even likes to answer the door for trick-or-treaters,* she thought, licking her lips. *And I don't think she ever helped carve a pumpkin—* "But what if she doesn't like it?" she asked.

Jessica hefted both boxes up on her shoulder and began to work her way toward the checkout counter. "Well, we'll grow into it eventually," she said. "And anyway, she's going to love it."

She turned around and gave Elizabeth a conspiratorial wink.

"Trust me!" she said, and then dissolved into the crowd.

Elizabeth sighed and turned her attention back to the rack with the colonial dress.

She hoped Jessica was right about the movie star costume.

She could really see her mother liking it.

And yet—

For some reason that she couldn't quite put her finger on, Elizabeth had a bad feeling about the whole thing.

Six

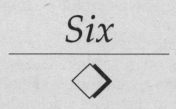

"We're going to dress up in *what?*" Joe Howell's eyes opened very wide.

"Well, you haven't let me finish," Steven pointed out. They were standing outside the costume store. Steven wondered if he'd made a fatal mistake by describing the nightgown part of the costume before talking about the makeup. "I mean, the real deal is going to be the makeup, know what I mean?" He leaned forward as Joe began to drift away. "It's going to be totally awesome," he said, sidestepping so Joe couldn't escape. "Totally awesome," he repeated.

Joe just shook his head. "There is no possible way I'm walking around town with some flowered nightgown on," he said, fixing Steven with a look.

Steven sighed. "First of all, no one's going to know it's us," he pointed out. "And second of all—" He paused, wondering what a second reason might be. *Aha!* "Second of all, we could wait to put the nightgowns on till it's time to scare the kids, if you want."

Joe hesitated.

"Come on, man!" Steven argued. "They'd never know it's us, anyway. They'll be screaming from here to the other side of the world, and you know it." The thought made him smile. "See, my sisters think they're being chased by a real monster, OK? One look, that's all it's going to take."

Joe grunted. Steven hoped that was a good sign.

"We'll call out the newspapers," he said jokingly. "The TV news shows. It's going to be the greatest scare of the century. Of *any* century."

Joe raised his eyebrow just a little. "Good luck, Wakefield. But count me out. What else did you have in mind besides nightgowns, anyway—a pair of cute little bunny slippers?"

Steven felt his face redden. He forced a laugh. "Bunny slippers? Ha ha! You've got to be kidding." Wearing only one bunny slipper was much cooler these days, that was for sure.

But he decided not to say that to Joe.

*　　　*　　　*

"I thought your dad wasn't coming till Halloween!" Jessica said in surprise.

The twins were sitting in the Riccolis' living room. They'd decided to stop at the old mansion on their way back from the mall. In the daylight, and with Eva Sullivan gone forever, the house was cheery and bright. The kids seemed well rested and happy too. It was obvious that no one had had any monster dreams all week.

"No, he came early," Juliana said happily. "It's like a Halloween present for us."

"Yeah, he showed up this morning," Andrew said. "Right in the middle of *Dancing Pink Elephants*—hey, Dad!"

"Did I hear my name?" Mr. Riccoli bustled down the heavy curving staircase into the living room and extended his hand to the twins. "I know I've met one of you," he said with a sheepish grin, "but I can't tell which one it was."

Elizabeth smiled back. "You met me," she volunteered. The last time Mr. Riccoli had been in town to visit, she and Todd had baby-sat the kids, and she'd gotten to know Mr. Riccoli a little. She liked him. He had a corny sense of humor a lot like her own father's. "This is my sister, Jessica."

"Nice to meet you," Jessica said. She stood up and shook Mr. Riccoli's hand.

"Charmed," Mr. Riccoli said, dropping into an extravagant bow. He winced as he straightened back up. "I used to be able to do that so well," he said ruefully. "But I haven't been the same since I busted my back on the rodeo circuit forty years ago."

Elizabeth couldn't help staring. If Mr. Riccoli had broken his back forty years before, how old would he be now? *He doesn't look much over thirty,* she thought. *But I guess it's hard to tell.* "I didn't know you were in rodeos, Mr. Riccoli," she said aloud.

Mr. Riccoli's eyes twinkled. "Yup," he said with a cowboy twang. "They used to call me Rodeo Rider Riccoli. Say that six times, real fast."

"Rodeo Rider Riccoli, Radio Rodeo Riddly—" Elizabeth began. She shook her head. "Sorry, I can barely even say it twice!"

"I didn't know you were in rodeos, Dad." Andrew stared up at his father in awe. "Did you ride a real bucking bronco?"

"And rope cows?" Gretchen chimed in.

"Aw, shucks," Mr. Riccoli said modestly. "Guess I just plumb forgot to tell you kids. Sure, I wore a ten-gallon hat and cowboy boots, and I rode broncos all over Texas. In my act I'd stand on one bronc's back and jump to another one."

"While they were *moving?*" Gretchen leaned forward with excitement.

"Oh, sure," Mr. Riccoli answered with a careless wave of his arm. "Forty, fifty, sixty miles an hour."

"Cool!" Andrew exclaimed.

"Wasn't that dangerous?" Olivia asked, her eyes wide.

"Well, of course it was dangerous," Mr. Riccoli said. "How do you think I broke my back? See, while I was in the air one day, jumping the thirty yards from one horse to the other, a gust of wind caught me." He shrugged. "Well, it wasn't an ordinary gust of wind, it was more like a tornado, but it carried me twenty miles and dumped me flat on my back in the middle of the desert."

"Awesome," Andrew whispered.

Jessica nudged Elizabeth. "Wow," she mouthed.

Elizabeth took a deep breath. No doubt about it, this was one of the most amazing stories she had ever heard.

"How did you get to the hospital?" Gretchen asked.

Mr. Riccoli shrugged. "Crawled," he explained. "Crawled for three days and nights nonstop, with a broken back. And as soon as I got out of that hospital, I hopped right back on my bronc."

Elizabeth's head was whirling with ideas. Maybe she could interview Mr. Riccoli for the *Sweet Valley Sixers*, the sixth-grade newspaper she edited. Maybe she could write her own adventure series based on his story. Maybe—

"My outfit's upstairs," Mr. Riccoli went on. "Cowboy hat, six-gun, boots, work shirt—hey, they didn't call me Rodeo Rider Riccoli for nothing, you know."

"Upstairs? Can we *see* it?" Andrew breathed.

"In a few days, son, in a few days." Mr. Riccoli held out his hands. "Anyway, that's why my back doesn't work so great."

"Wow," Gretchen said, her eyes shining.

"Wait till I tell the other kids!" Andrew said.

Jessica turned to Elizabeth, a big grin on her face. "I bet this guy is *famous*," she whispered with excitement.

"Daddy?" Juliana was staring at her father with a frown. "There's one thing I don't understand. Remember last summer when we were on vacation and I wanted to go horseback riding? And they said I was too little but I could go with you?" She wrinkled her nose. "And I really, really wanted to go, but you said you didn't know how to ride horses and you were scared to death of them? Remember, Daddy?"

Suddenly the room was very quiet. Elizabeth

frowned. Now that she thought about it, the story seemed a little unbelievable. *How far could you actually jump from one bucking bronco to another?* she wondered. Somehow she didn't think it was thirty yards.

"That's right, Dad, I remember that too," Olivia said after a moment. "So what's this about Mr. Rodeo Roper Ripper Whatever, huh?" She arched her eyebrows and stared at her father.

Gretchen pointed at her father accusingly. "This wasn't one of your made-up stories again, was it?"

Mr. Riccoli grinned. "Guilty," he admitted.

Elizabeth couldn't help laughing. She was a little embarrassed that she believed his story in the first place. Of course it couldn't have been true. For one thing, Mr. Riccoli wasn't old enough. For another

Jessica leaned over. "I knew it all along," she whispered proudly. "No way anyone could crawl three days across the desert with a broken back."

"Aw, I knew it all along," Gretchen said loudly. "A tornado couldn't carry you twenty miles."

"So did I," Andrew boasted. "A bucking bronco would throw Dad off in a *second*. In *half* a second. Remember how he almost fell off the merry-go-round that one time?" He grinned at his father. "And that stuff about the cowboy outfit—"

"Well, wait a minute," Mr. Riccoli said, interrupting. "That part happens to be true." He stuck out his lower lip. "No one in my family ever believes me," he said mournfully, looking at Elizabeth. "You can't imagine how much that hurts."

Elizabeth giggled. That was exactly the kind of thing her father liked to say.

"Well, if you wouldn't *lie* all the time," Olivia said with emphasis.

"Yeah, if you would just stop telling us you were a pirate, or an astronaut, or a giraffe—" Andrew added.

"But I *do* have a cowboy outfit," Mr. Riccoli went on, winking at Elizabeth. "Cross my heart and all that jazz. And I'll show you kids in a few days."

Juliana's hand flew up to her mouth. "Halloween!"

"Oween!" Nate put in.

"Oween!" Mr. Riccoli echoed his youngest son. He grabbed Nate up in a bear hug. "Your mama and I have been invited to a Halloween party," he said, rubbing Nate's nose with his own. "And we're going as cowboy and cowgirl—the Rootin'-Tootin', Ramblin'-Scramblin' Roughneck Riccolis, that's us." His eyes crinkled into a smile. "*If* we can get baby-sitters. So how about it?" He faced the twins. "You two interested?"

Elizabeth and Jessica exchanged glances. Elizabeth knew her sister was thinking the same thing she was:

With no monster around, this house is a lot of fun!

"You bet!" she said as Jessica nodded in agreement.

Seven

"But what if she doesn't like it?" Elizabeth whispered.

"Trust me," Jessica whispered back, wondering why they were whispering. The twins were on the front porch of their house, having just gotten home from the Riccolis'. Jessica hefted her packages from one hand to the other. "It's the best costume in the world," she declared. "Mom is going to love it. Trust me." She reached for the door handle.

"Every time you say 'trust me,' I feel like I have humongous butterflies flying around in my stomach," Elizabeth said.

"Well, stop asking me stupid questions, and maybe I'll stop saying 'trust me'!" Jessica hissed back. In fact, her own stomach felt full of butterflies. Buying the movie star costume for her mother to wear on Halloween had seemed like a great idea at the time. Now that they were out of the store, though, Jessica had a sneaking suspicion that her mother wouldn't exactly be thrilled.

She glared at her sister. "What are you waiting for?" she asked. "Go on in!"

"I can't," Elizabeth replied. "You're blocking the way."

"Whatever," Jessica muttered. She flung open the door. "Mom? We're home!"

There was no answer.

"Mom?" Jessica hung up her jacket. "Mom?"

"In here," Mrs. Wakefield called from the living room. "Did you have fun? Did you buy anything?"

Jessica bustled in. Her mother was sitting on the couch, reading a magazine. "Here you go!" Jessica said proudly, pulling her mother's costume out of its bag and holding it up.

"A movie star costume," Mrs. Wakefield said with a nod. "Very nice. You'll look sweet in it, Jessica."

"What did I tell you?" Elizabeth whispered from behind, putting a hand on Jessica's shoulder.

"She never wears a costume, doofus," Jessica whispered back. "Of *course* she thinks it's for me." She put on her most bubbly voice, the better to convince her mother. "Actually, Mom, this isn't for me. It's for you!"

"For me?" Mrs. Wakefield's eyes widened.

Jessica frowned. "Yeah. For you."

Mrs. Wakefield looked suddenly pale. "Oh."

Jessica's frown deepened. That "oh" had sounded awfully flat. Almost as if her mother had butterflies in her own stomach.

"Yeah, it's yours, Mom," Elizabeth said from beside Jessica. She flashed Jessica a look that said, "Why didn't you listen to me?"

"Isn't it gorgeous, Mom?" Jessica asked, trying hard to ignore her sister. "You'll look great. You'll feel, like, thirty years younger. I mean, twenty years younger. I mean, ten years older—" No, that wasn't exactly right either. "Trust me," she said at last, giving a little laugh. "You'll feel great is all."

Mrs. Wakefield's eyes seemed to cloud over. "You know I don't like to dress up on Halloween," she said in a soft voice.

And before Jessica could stop her, Mrs. Wakefield stood up from the couch and left the room.

"But *why* doesn't Mom like to dress up on Halloween?" Elizabeth asked, flopping down on the living room sofa. Now that she thought about it, she realized that Mrs. Wakefield had never even taken the twins trick-or-treating when they were young.

Jessica sighed. "Beats me," she said. Her fingers tapped out an irregular rhythm on the costume box. The girls were talking in low voices so their mother wouldn't hear—wherever she was. "All I can figure is—"

"What?" Elizabeth asked curiously.

"Oh—nothing." Jessica let the box drop to the floor. She sank down onto the couch. "It's almost like—like something happened to her once on Halloween. You know, a long time ago. And she's never really gotten over it."

Elizabeth considered. "You mean, like, a traumatic experience? Like when we were in kindergarten and we went to see the fireworks show at the park?" Elizabeth still remembered that show as if it were yesterday. One of the fireworks had exploded with a huge bang, sending her running to her parents for comfort. For weeks afterward loud noises had terrified her.

Jessica frowned. "Maybe. Maybe some kid stole her candy bag when she was little. Or maybe—" She scratched her head thoughtfully. "I don't know. Maybe some kid in a vampire costume scared her out of her wits when she was, like, three."

Elizabeth frowned. "If someone stole your

candy, would that make you never want to celebrate Halloween again?"

"Not really," Jessica admitted. "But maybe—you know. Maybe it was something worse." She stood up quickly. "I'm going over to Secca Lake with some of the Unicorns. Catch you later."

"Have fun," Elizabeth mumbled. But she wasn't really listening to her sister. She dropped onto a chair, wondering.

Wondering what could happen to a kid on Halloween besides having her bag of candy stolen. Or being frightened by a big kid in a vampire costume.

And wondering what possibly could have happened to her mother to make her hate Halloween so very much.

"Isn't this incredibly wonderful?" Jessica trailed a bare foot in the cool, still waters of Secca Lake and leaned back in the canoe. In the stern of the canoe Jessica's sort-of boyfriend, Aaron Dallas, was whistling cheerfully. Jessica breathed a deep sigh. Out here, in the sunshine and fresh air, it was hard to be worried about Eva Sullivan.

Or mothers who didn't like Halloween.

She looked at her friends scattered around the lake. All the girls were in the Unicorn Club, a group of girls who considered themselves to be the prettiest and most popular at Sweet Valley

Middle School. Janet Howell, the president of the Unicorn Club, and Denny Jacobson, her sort-of boyfriend, were in a rowboat near the middle of the lake. Kimberly Haver and Grace Oliver were listening to a Johnny Buck tape near the dock, and over on the beach Jessica could see Ellen Riteman, Mandy Miller, and a few other kids hitting a volleyball.

"Hey, Jessica!" Lila Fowler called out. Jessica turned to see her best friend in the bow of a red canoe, with Jake Hamilton paddling along behind her. "I've been looking for you."

Jessica smiled lazily. The water felt wonderful against her toes. "Well, here I am!" she said.

Slowly the canoes drifted toward each other. Jessica could hear a faint thud as their sides came together. Tiny waves rolled gently between the boats. "Oh, Aaron!" Lila put her hands on her hips and rolled her eyes. "Watch where you're going, *please.*"

"Yeah, Aaron." Jake put his hands on his own hips. "Watch where you're going, Aaron." He started to laugh.

"What are you talking about?" Aaron stared hard at Lila. "It was *you* guys who—"

Lila sighed loudly. "Oh, well, never mind," she said, grinning at Jake as if they shared some big secret. She leaned back and squeezed his hand. "Listen, Jessica," she said sharply. "A little birdie told me that you aren't trick-or-treating with the Unicorns on Halloween."

Jessica frowned. "What are you talking about? Of course I'm trick-or-treating with you guys."

Lila raised an eyebrow. "That's not what *I* heard," she informed Jessica. "*I* heard you were *baby-sitting.*"

"Well, I'm doing both," she said, a little defensively. "I don't have to baby-sit till late and—"

"Are you baby-sitting too, Aaron?" Jake asked in a silly, high-pitched voice, catching Lila's eye.

"Who, me?" Aaron looked horrified at the idea.

"Well, you'll have to start baby-sitting *pretty* late if you want to go trick-or-treating with us," Lila went on, staring Jessica right in the eye. "You know we won't even *start* trick-or-treating till about nine. And then there's the party. Don't tell me you're going to miss the biggest party of the year to *baby-sit.*"

Jessica stiffened. "*What* party?"

"Oh, I didn't tell you?" Lila asked breezily. "I'm throwing a Halloween party. At my place."

Jessica felt her stomach knot. Lila was the richest girl in Sweet Valley, and she took every opportunity to show people, especially Jessica, how lucky she was. She lived in a gorgeous mansion and threw really amazing parties. Jessica was starting to think that she'd made exactly the wrong decision about baby-sitting. But there was no way she was going to show Lila that. "Well, if I have to miss the party, then I miss the party," she snapped. "That wouldn't be the worst thing in the world."

But what if it is? What if I'm missing the greatest party of my life? What if the Unicorns cut me dead? Suddenly the water felt cold on her leg. Sitting up, she pulled her foot back into the canoe.

"Baby-sitting," Lila repeated. She stole a look back at Jake, who shook his head in mock disgust. Lila exploded into gales of laughter. "Baby-sitting? I mean, come on, Jessica. It's Halloween!"

"I know it's Halloween," Jessica snarled. She dipped her paddle into the water and stroked vigorously. The canoe shot forward. "Come on, Aaron, let's get out of here," she hissed under her breath.

"We'll miss you!" Lila exclaimed in a voice that sounded a little too bright to be genuine.

"Some of us have to *work* for a living!" Jessica called back over her shoulder. She knew it wasn't the best comeback in the world, but it was all she could think of.

"Oh, Jessica." From behind her Jessica could hear Lila snicker. "Why don't you get a life, huh?"

Angrily Jessica plunged her oar through the water again. It felt good. But she half wished she were jabbing the paddle into her so-called friend instead of into the lake.

"'Why don't you watch where you're going, Aaron?'" Behind her Jessica could hear Aaron mimicking Lila's breathy voice. He dropped his paddle into the boat. "Yeah, right."

They had paddled about a hundred yards from Lila's canoe, but Jessica still could hear Lila's laughter resounding across the still waters of the lake. Her shoulders felt sore. She dropped her own paddle into the boat too, not caring where it landed. "What are you doing for Halloween?" Jessica asked curiously, trying not to think about Lila.

Aaron snorted. "Well, I was *planning* to go with some of my buddies," he said. "Like that clown Jake Hamilton over there." He jabbed an angry forefinger in Jake and Lila's direction. "But now I'm not so sure."

"They're pretty annoying, all right," Jessica agreed. She shaded her eyes and stared toward the other boat. Lila wasn't bothering to paddle at all. She was just sitting there, looking deep into Jake's eyes. Jessica squirmed with irritation.

Aaron cleared his throat. "Hey, Jess!" he stage-whispered. "What do you say we go ram into Lila and Jake?"

"Hey, yeah!" Jessica grinned. "But let's not

ram into them," she whispered back. "Let's just give them a scare. OK?"

"Sure," Aaron agreed. The canoe glided swiftly forward. Jessica pulled her own paddle through the water and watched the lake swirl around it.

"Less noise." Aaron's voice was soft.

Jessica concentrated on being quiet. *Let's pretend,* she thought, remembering a game she and Elizabeth had loved to play when they were younger. *Let's pretend that I'm a tiger and I'm sneaking up on you and . . .* She dipped the paddle back into the water and pulled as smoothly as she could. A few stray bubbles popped to the surface, but there was no noise at all. Gently Jessica shifted her weight.

Behind her a paddle clunked heavily against the side of the boat. "Less noise," Jessica hissed, trying not to laugh.

"Sor-ry," Aaron muttered.

Jake and Lila were only about twenty feet away. Jessica leaned back. "When I say 'now,'" she whispered, "we'll pretend we're out of control, OK?" Without waiting for an answer, she started to count. "One . . . two . . . three . . . *now!*"

Together she and Aaron screamed hysterically. Jessica gave one last stroke with her paddle, then held it out in front of her like a sword. "We're out of control!" she yelled at the top of her lungs.

"The engine's busted!" Aaron screeched.

Jake and Lila stiffened and turned to look. Their eyes grew big. "Help!" Lila shouted, ducking back against the side. Her canoe rocked furiously.

"Stop!" Jake shouted, reaching for his paddle.

"Out of the way!" Aaron cried in a panicky voice.

"We're trying!" Jake looked terrified. When he couldn't locate his paddle, he plunged his arm into the water and began thrashing it around furiously. At the same time Lila shut her eyes, stood up, and began to bawl.

"Sit down!" Jake cried out. "You'll tip us—"

For a split second Lila teetered on the edge of her canoe. Then she flung her arms back and started to fall. With an anguished cry she hit the water and disappeared.

Aaron thrust his paddle into the water and braked the boat. "Oh, my," he said innocently. "Gee whiz, Jessica, look what happened to Lila!"

Lila's face broke the surface of the lake. "Get me out—" she yelled before swallowing a mouthful of water. "Get me out of here!" she sputtered. "Now!"

"Goodness gracious," Jessica said, opening her eyes very wide and putting her hand to her cheek in mock amazement. She held the end of her paddle toward Lila. "Why, Lila! I didn't know you were planning to go swimming today!"

Lila stared daggers at Jessica, but she caught the end of the paddle and let herself be pulled toward her canoe. "I bet you did that on purpose, Jessica Wakefield!" she said.

"Who, me?" Jessica blinked hard.

"Why don't you watch where you're going, Jake?" Aaron asked. Together he and Jessica managed to get Lila back into her canoe. "I mean, we were yelling like crazy, but you guys never even turned around."

"I guess you were too busy with each other," Jessica added. She dipped her paddle back into the water and gazed up at the blue sky. "Well, we'll see you later."

Lila huddled against the side of the canoe, a scowl on her face. Her hair was a mess, and rivers of water were streaming down her clothes. "What am I supposed to do now?" she wailed.

"Change your clothes, I guess," Aaron said with a shrug, backpaddling to turn the canoe around.

"But this is genuine Belle da Costa swimwear!" Lila cried, motioning to her sodden outfit. "It cost my dad, like, eight hundred dollars, and it's not supposed to get wet!"

"Oh, Lila," Jessica said, putting on her most sympathetic face. "You really should be more careful!"

*   *   *

"So the world is finally back to normal." Jessica sighed as she prepared for bed that night. "No monsters at the Riccoli house. I had a great time at Secca Lake. I'm not even worrying about Mom anymore." She perched on the edge of Elizabeth's desk. "I mean, Mom's a grown-up, right? She can take care of herself."

"Uh-huh." Elizabeth yawned. She'd had a busy day too. She'd finished another Jane Austen novel, *Persuasion*, and she'd loved every single word.

"Anyway—" Jessica picked up Elizabeth's copy of *Persuasion* and started to leaf through it. "I feel totally safe again. Guess the whole thing with Eva Sullivan was just in our imaginations."

Elizabeth looked down at the scratches on her wrist. She winced, remembering how the monster's claws had dug into her flesh as she hung over the parapet of the Riccolis' roof not all that many days ago. The scratches had faded, but she could still see a few angry red welts, and a long, swollen white line ran almost up to the palm of her hand.

"Elizabeth!"

Elizabeth looked up with a start. "Hmm? What?"

"I *said*, don't you think the monster was all in our imaginations?" Jessica asked, staring at Elizabeth intently.

Gently Elizabeth stroked the long white scratch on her wrist, not wanting to look at it anymore. She took a deep breath, noticing that her ribs were still a little painful from where she had swung against the side of the house—

If she had swung against the side of the house.

"E-liz-a-beth!" Jessica sounded exasperated. "It was all in our imaginations, wasn't it?"

Slowly Elizabeth nodded. Her neck and shoulder throbbed faintly, and she remembered how sore they had been a week or so ago, the last time they had baby-sat the Riccoli kids—

"Yeah," she said, pushing that night firmly out of her mind.

She gave a careless laugh.

"I mean, what other explanation could there be?"

Eight

◇

Jessica opened her eyes. Darkness, darkness all around her. Leaning a fraction of an inch to the left, she glanced at the digital clock on her bed-side table. 2:57.

No wonder it was so dark.

With a deep sigh Jessica wrapped her arms around her pillow and shifted position. Her leg itched, so she scratched it, her fingernails scraping pleasantly against her skin. She yawned and tried to make her mind a perfect blank.

The bed creaked.

Jessica opened one eye ever so slightly. *Ignore it,* she told herself. She concentrated on the rising and falling of her chest. *Breathe in. Now out. Breathe in—*

Her leg itched again. Shaking her head,

she scratched it and checked the clock once more. 2:59.

This time she flopped onto her back. Resting against the pillow, she relaxed one muscle at a time, beginning with her toes. *This ought to do it,* she thought as a great wave of sleepiness washed over her. *Yup.* Slowly she flexed the muscles in her ankles and let them go. Already she could feel herself drifting back to sleep again.

Scritch. Scratch. Scritch.

In the darkness Jessica's eyes flew open. The noise had sounded like the sound she'd made when scratching her legs. But she hadn't scratched her legs. Had she?

She flexed her fingers just to make sure.

Scritch. Scratch. Scritch! The noise was louder.

Jessica jerked her head, her heart beating furiously. The sound was coming from the window. She blinked hard, hoping to catch a faint glimpse of the curtains in the dim moonlight. Something was out there at the window. Something.

Scritch.

Jessica swung her legs over the bed and set her feet down silently on the floor. Her palms felt moist. *What could possibly be scratching at my window at three o'clock in the morning?* she wondered. As her eyes became accustomed to the darkness Jessica sat still as still.

The sound stopped.

There's nothing there, Jessica told herself at last, feeling almost embarrassed. *Nothing at all, you wimp!* Taking a deep breath, she was ready to tumble back into bed again when the pale moonlight suddenly brightened.

And in a flash Jessica saw—or thought she saw—a familiar, gruesome figure standing outside her window.

A figure with half a face.

A girl.

Wearing a nightgown.

A scream began to rise in Jessica's throat, but she bit it off angrily. *It can't be!* she shouted to herself, feeling the blood pounding through her temples. *The monster is gone! She's gone. . . .* Violently she squeezed her eyes shut, seeing little flecks of blue, red, and yellow explode. *Stay calm,* she ordered herself.

There was total silence.

Hardly daring to breathe, Jessica opened her eyes as slowly as she could. The moonlight was dim once more. Jessica stared toward the window, prepared for the worst.

But the window was empty now.

Jessica felt herself exhale. Wearily she laid her head back on her pillow and shut her eyes again. Obviously her eyes had been playing tricks on her. She considered getting up to check the window, but she decided she'd better not. *It's not that*

I'm scared, she reminded herself. *It's just that . . . tomorrow's a busy day. I need my sleep. That's all.*

Slowly her heartbeat returned to normal.

And in a few minutes Jessica was sound asleep once more.

"Want a banana in yours?" Elizabeth asked her sister the next morning. She was preparing cereal for herself, and the bananas looked ripe to perfection.

Jessica started. "Huh?"

Elizabeth glanced at Jessica with surprise. "Just wondering if you want me to cut some bananas for your cereal, that's all." She sliced off quarter-size pieces of the yellow fruit. "You don't have to look at me like you've seen a ghost!"

Jessica turned pale. "A ghost?" She laughed lightly. "Oh. No, no, thanks. Don't worry about me." Drumming her fingers on the table, she dipped her spoon into her cup and scooped up some orange juice.

"Jessica!" Elizabeth shook her head. What was up with her sister today? "That isn't a bowl!"

"It isn't?" Jessica looked down at her cup. "Oh. I mean, yeah. I—I kind of knew that."

Elizabeth raised her eyebrows. "So you knew that wasn't your bowl. Does that mean you've decided to drink orange juice with a spoon?"

Jessica reddened. *"No,"* she said emphatically.

She thrust her spoon into her bowl of cereal so forcefully, droplets of milk flew across the table.

Elizabeth studied her sister with a frown. Jessica's face looked blotchy, she noticed, as if she hadn't slept well, and her eyes seemed very far away. "Are you all right?" she asked, neatly slicing the last section of banana. The knife made a little scratching sound as it slid across the cutting board.

Jessica gasped. "What was that?"

"My knife, I guess," Elizabeth said. She set the knife down and touched Jessica on the shoulder. "Are you *really* OK?" she asked with concern.

"I'm fine." Jessica took a deep breath. Her lips curved upward into a huge smile. "Really. Just— too much canoeing yesterday, that's all." She laughed.

Elizabeth looked at her twin skeptically. "Well . . . OK."

But she wished Jessica's laugh had sounded less—forced.

And she wished that when Jessica's mouth had smiled, her eyes had smiled too.

Let's see, Elizabeth said to herself that night. She lay in her dark bedroom, thinking herself to sleep. *What stories should I put into the* Sixers *this week?*

With a yawn she turned to face the window.

Amy's article about the new cafeteria cooks, she thought drowsily. *They can't be worse than the old ones! And the article about the kids who sing over at the nursing home—now who wrote that one?*

Her mind drew a blank.

Well, it doesn't matter, she thought, and she yawned again. Thoughts tumbled around slowly in her brain, the way they always did just before she went to sleep. One second she was wondering if she'd packed her schoolbag. The next she was humming a little snatch of a Johnny Buck tune to herself. She stretched.

Then suddenly the ghastly face of the Riccolis' monster flashed into her mind. *Ugh,* Elizabeth thought, waiting for her mind to switch to another *Sixers* idea. Then she realized that there was a reason why she was thinking about Eva Sullivan's face.

Something that looked just like it was staring in through her window!

Oh, man! Elizabeth's blood curdled. With a quick motion she scurried out of bed, feet padding onto the carpet. *It can't be—it can't be.* Blinking furiously, she stared out toward the window, daring the monster to be there—

But it wasn't.

Outside, the shadow of a tree swayed gently in the breeze. *That's all it was,* Elizabeth assured herself, feeling her pulse return to normal. *Just a tree. And my imagination playing tricks on me again.*

Elizabeth felt embarrassed to have made such a fuss about a tree. She stood watching for another ten or twenty seconds, but nothing unusual happened. Taking a deep breath, she climbed back into bed and pulled the covers up to her chin.

The shadow must have moved so fast, it fooled me into thinking it was a different shape, she told herself. *But it wasn't a face. How could I have thought anything so stupid?*

Closing her eyes tightly, Elizabeth rolled over and turned her face to the wall.

Before long she was sound asleep.

"That is the biggest grapefruit I have ever seen in my life," Jessica said the next morning. She leaned against the counter and watched Steven viciously peeling the fruit with his bare hands. She had trouble imagining that even her always hungry brother could eat something so humongous all by himself.

Juice caught Steven squarely in the eye. "It's a monster, isn't it?" he crowed happily.

Elizabeth's head snapped up. "What did you say?" She leaned across the table, staring at Steven, a stricken look on her face.

"A monster grapefruit," Steven explained, raising his eyebrows. "I just meant it was big.

Hey! You don't suppose this really is a grapefruit monsters eat, do you?" He grinned and ran his tongue tenderly around his lips. "Aha! Eet ees a grapefruit for me, ze fearsome monster of Sveet Valley!"

"You sound totally ridiculous," Jessica said with a sigh. "Did you want a grapefruit, Lizzie?"

"What?" Elizabeth swept some strands of hair off her face and peered up at Jessica, confused. "What did you say?"

Jessica frowned. "Elizabeth, are you all right?" she demanded. Her twin didn't seem to be exactly together this morning.

"My sister all right?" Steven grunted, tearing off three sections of grapefruit and stuffing them into his mouth. "You have *got* to be kidding."

Jessica decided to ignore her brother. "Are you OK?" she repeated.

"Fine," Elizabeth said quickly, then lowered her eyes.

Jessica shook her head. She rested a hand on her sister's shoulder, the way Elizabeth had done the previous morning. "Are you sure?"

Elizabeth bit her lip. "Well—um—I had a dream last night."

"A dream?" Jessica repeated. "Tell me."

"Oooh, I had a dream too," Steven sang out. "I dreamed I was a beagle out hunting rabbits and—"

"Never mind," Elizabeth said thickly. She plastered a weak grin on her face. "I thought I saw a face at my window. *You* know. But it was just a dream."

Jessica thought she did know. "The crooked nose?" she asked. "And the scars?"

"Well—" Elizabeth considered. "I—I don't know for sure," she admitted. "It was just a fraction of a second, and I was, like, too far away to see really well and—" She shook her head vehemently. "But it couldn't have been," she said in a stronger tone of voice.

"I had a dream like that too," Jessica said slowly. "Not last night. The night before." The details seemed unusually clear for a dream that was already more than a day old. "Nightgown and everything. But I was just dreaming, of course," she said, giving a little forced laugh. "I've had Eva Sullivan on the brain so long, I can't stop thinking about her."

Elizabeth nodded thoughtfully. "Me too, I guess. I mean, of course."

Steven was watching his sisters carefully. "You saw that ghost? Here? Last night?" he asked. "How come you guys get all the fun?"

"Oh, be quiet, Steven," Jessica muttered.

"Is this the monster that goes around carrying a stuffed rabbit?" Steven wanted to know. He ripped off another chunk of grapefruit. "O Thumper,

Thumper, wherefore art thou, Thumper?" he asked in a silly voice. "Thought that one only showed up at the Riccolis' house."

"Teddy bear," Jessica corrected him automatically. "And it doesn't have the teddy bear anymore. It lost it."

"It *what?*" Steven made a face.

"It *lost* it," Jessica repeated. "The bear's in my closet now. . . ." Her voice trailed off. She took a deep breath and looked around the bright, sunny kitchen. The whole thing was ridiculous. Totally ridiculous. There were no such things as monsters anyway. And the idea of a monster losing its teddy bear—

"Too stupid for words," Jessica muttered aloud. She spread out her arms and smiled at her sister. "It's only Halloween butterflies. It can't be real."

"Of course not," Elizabeth echoed her. "Our imaginations are just running away with us, that's all." But she didn't quite meet her sister's gaze.

"It was probably nothing," Jessica agreed. Standing up from the table, she reached for her book bag.

"If you're already this scared," Steven observed, spitting a grapefruit seed halfway across the table, "just wait till Halloween. You'll be begging for mercy." He let out a horrible cackling noise.

"Cut it out, Steven," Jessica ordered, feeling her stomach doing flip-flops.

Steven leered at her. "No, seriously," he said. "How many scars were there on the monster's face, anyway? Four? Five?"

Jessica considered. The trouble was, it was kind of hard to tell where one scar ended and the next began. "Probably five—" She broke off with a frown. "Why do you care?" she asked.

Steven shrugged. "Oh, well, you know," he said grandly. "I'm, like, doing research for a school project. I'm writing a paper on, um, scars in literature."

Jessica snorted.

"Sisters never understand their genius brothers," Steven remarked, accidentally knocking the sugar bowl on the floor. "It's a scientifically proven fact."

Jessica paused on her way to the front door. "Oh, I understand that you're a genius, all right."

Steven's eyes widened. "You do?"

"Yup," Jessica replied as she opened the door. "In your dreams, that is."

Nine

"There's no reason to go to bed now," Elizabeth said, sipping from her cup of hot chocolate. It was very late that evening, and the twins were sitting alone in the kitchen. She played with a spoon and tried hard not to yawn.

"That is so true," Jessica agreed, staring intently into her own cup. "I mean, the night's just starting."

"Yeah." Elizabeth opened her eyes very wide. "And we're just having such a great conversation, Jess, I feel like we have to stay up till it's over."

"Uh-huh," Jessica said. She nodded and repeated herself a little louder. "Uh-huh!"

Elizabeth sneaked a quick look at the kitchen clock. Eleven forty-five—way past her normal

bedtime. "We sure do have the best conversations, don't we, Jessica?" she asked brightly, wondering what they had just been talking about.

"We sure do." Jessica smiled faintly at her sister.

There was a pause. Elizabeth put down the
spoon and toyed nervously with the handle of
her cup. "So how about those Bulls, huh?" she
asked in her breeziest tone of voice.

Jessica made a face. "We already talked about
basketball, Lizzie."

"Really?" Elizabeth had forgotten. It seemed
like ages had gone by since they'd sat down for a
quick cup of hot chocolate. She had a sneaking
suspicion that they'd already talked about every
possible subject.

Except one, of course.

Eva Sullivan, silhouetted—in dreams or reality—against their very own windows.

"Well—um—" Elizabeth frowned. "Wasn't
that a great dinner tonight?"

"Oh, yeah," Jessica agreed with feeling. Taking
a deep breath, she grinned across at Elizabeth.
"Don't you just love croutons in your salad?"

"And that awesome ranch dressing!"
Elizabeth added, trying hard to remember what
else they'd had.

"And what terrific orange juice," Jessica
put in.

Elizabeth stretched out her toes and relaxed. As long as they could remember the entire dinner menu, this conversation looked good for five minutes at least.

". . . so there's Charlie Cashman and then Brian Boyd," Elizabeth was saying. "I mean, actually, I guess Brian would come before Charlie, wouldn't he?"

Jessica was so tired, she could barely keep her eyes open. "Um, yeah," she said, struggling to remember what they were talking about. *Oh, yeah. Putting our classmates' names in alphabetical order,* she thought. *That's right.* "Yeah," she said. "*B* comes before *C.*" She was sure she'd rather fall asleep at the table than go to bed. Anything would be better than lying there in the darkness waiting to see if . . . something . . . would happen.

"And then who?" Elizabeth yawned, quickly covering her mouth. "I can't imagine why I'm so tired!" She gave a nervous little laugh.

I can, Jessica thought. She looked at the hands of the clock, creeping slowly toward twelve. She remembered many evenings when she'd been younger, when she'd begged her parents to let her stay up till midnight. Staying up late wasn't all it was cracked up to be, that was for sure. "How about some more hot chocolate?" she asked, standing up and feeling a little dizzy.

. For a brief instant Elizabeth looked faintly sick. But she held out her cup. "Um—yeah," she said slowly. "I think that would be a good idea."

Jessica crossed the room to the microwave. Setting the cups down on the counter, she turned to her sister. "Regular or decaf?" she asked, and then she shook her head at her own stupidity. *Am I zonked or what?* "I mean, sugar free or—"

"Jessica!" Elizabeth half rose in her chair. Slowly she pointed a trembling finger toward the sliding glass door that led to the porch. *"Look!"*

"What?" Jessica felt the blood drain from her face. She whirled around and stared at the door. She was wide awake for the first time in what seemed like hours.

"I saw—I saw—" Elizabeth gestured helplessly at the door.

Jessica stood stock-still. She couldn't see a thing—until, out of the corner of her eye, she caught sight of a sudden movement.

There was a flash of light.

And a twisted and bruised fist beat down heavily against the pane of glass.

"Oh, man!" Jessica felt as if someone had grabbed her from behind. She had never been so terrified in her entire life. Without thinking, she opened her mouth to scream. But she couldn't hear her own voice. Instead a terrible hammering resounded in her ears. Two noises, beating as if they were one: The pounding of the monster on the door.

And the pounding of her own heart inside her chest.

"Elizabeth? Jessica?"

Brandishing an empty pop bottle, Mr. Wakefield charged into the kitchen. "What's going on?" he asked in a hoarse, froggy voice.

"Dad!" Elizabeth had never been so glad to see her father. She dashed into his welcoming arms and buried her face against the old familiar cloth of his bathrobe. "Is it gone?" she asked, almost afraid to move.

"Is what gone, sweetie?" Mr. Wakefield asked.

Elizabeth let out a shuddering sob. In her mind's eye she could still see Eva Sullivan at the door, beating on the pane of glass, her mouth twisted into a hideous, evil smile. "The—the monster." Elizabeth pointed toward the door. "There was a horrible monster over there and—" She bit her lip to keep from crying.

"A monster?" Mr. Wakefield fixed Elizabeth with a look.

Jessica pointed to the door. "Look for—you know. Scratch marks."

"Scratch marks?" Mr. Wakefield flicked on the floodlight that illuminated the porch. He studied the backyard while the two girls huddled together.

Elizabeth took a deep breath and held her twin tightly. The sight of the monster was still fresh in her mind. "You must have screamed loudly enough to wake Dad," she said in a very small voice.

Jessica could only nod.

"Nothing out here," Mr. Wakefield announced, still clutching the bottle. He frowned. "Listen, girls, are you sure you saw something?"

Elizabeth took a deep breath. "Yes," she said, the word coming out squeakier than she would have liked.

"Yes," Jessica confirmed in a voice no louder than a sigh.

Mr. Wakefield stared from one to the other and back. "All right," he said gruffly. "I don't know about monsters. But if someone is running around my property at—" He turned and checked the clock. "At twelve-oh-five in the morning, I want to know about it." He unlocked the glass door and pulled it open. "Be right back." And he stepped out into the night.

Twelve-oh-five. Elizabeth's head spun. The whole thing had taken less than five minutes. Probably way less than five minutes. It had seemed like forever. *Good thing the door was locked. And a good thing Jessica screamed as loudly as she did. And a good thing Eva didn't manage to break the door down.*

"Elizabeth?" Jessica sounded terrified.

Elizabeth reached for her sister's hand. Her heart was still beating furiously. She tried not to think of her father out in the darkness, armed with only a recyclable piece of plastic. "What is it?" she asked.

"She's not just in our dreams anymore," Jessica said, her face creased with tension. "She's—she's in reality now." Her eyes stared straight ahead. Elizabeth could see a few beads of sweat appear on her sister's forehead. "She's *here,* and she's going to kill us in our beds, and—"

"No way." But even as Elizabeth spoke, she felt her heart seize up with fear. *Jessica's right,* she told herself.

It was bad enough when the monster was only at the Riccolis'. And it was bad enough when she was only in their dreams. *But if she's going to terrorize us at our house, when we're wide awake—*

She decided not to finish her thought.

There was a sudden motion outside. Elizabeth froze. Then she breathed normally again as she recognized her father's bathrobe around the corner. Mr. Wakefield came in and shrugged.

"No sign of anything," he said, stifling a yawn. "Must have been a case of Halloween jitters, that's all. I'd suggest you two get some sleep."

He nudged the glass door shut behind him.

"But—" Jessica began. A worried look crept over her face.

"No buts." Mr. Wakefield turned off the flood-light. "It's long past your bedtime. The best cure for what ails you is sleep. Don't argue. Just go."

Elizabeth knew that her father meant what he said. She moved unwillingly toward the stairs. Then she remembered there was something she still had to do.

"Dad?" she asked slowly, swallowing hard. "Would you mind—you know, locking the door first?"

"But I just don't get it," Jessica whispered. The twins were holed up in Elizabeth's bed later that same night. They'd gotten their nightgowns on, but neither girl had dared to try going to sleep. Every sound made Elizabeth jump. "How did she escape from our nightmares?"

"I don't get it either," Elizabeth admitted. She slid her feet under the warm comforter. "It's al-most like—like we brought her back with us or something."

"But how could we have done that?" Jessica wanted to know.

Elizabeth shook her head. She felt very, very tired. "Maybe there's—you know, a bridge," she said, sketching one with her hand.

"A bridge?" Jessica looked baffled.

"Yeah, a bridge." Elizabeth wasn't sure she could explain it properly. "It's, like, here's us awake." She touched a corner of her night table. "And here's us asleep." She motioned to the bed. "See, they don't touch, right? It's sort of two different worlds."

"Uh-huh." Jessica nodded dubiously.

"But maybe there's some kind of invisible bridge that connects them," Elizabeth went on. Slowly she ran her hand from the table to the bed and back. "Maybe things can move between waking and sleeping. If they use the bridge."

"But who built the bridge?" Jessica demanded.

Elizabeth sighed. "I don't mean a real bridge, Jess." She considered. "Just—like a door—a way of getting from one world into another." She rubbed her eyes. Did that make any sense at all? "Maybe something we did opened that door."

"Or maybe—" Jessica clapped a hand over her mouth.

"What?" Elizabeth asked.

"Your last nightmare," Jessica said, her knuckles turning white. "Remember when you grabbed the monster by the wrist?"

How could I forget? "Yeah?" Elizabeth prompted her.

"Well, you woke up just then," Jessica said, swallowing hard. "Do you think maybe you could have, like, pulled her into this world with you?"

Elizabeth could see herself suspended from the Riccolis' roof, hanging on to Eva Sullivan's ghastly wrist for dear life. She could almost feel the puffy flesh between her fingers.

"I guess that could have happened," she said after a moment, picking imaginary threads off her pillow. "Only—I let go just before I woke up."

"Oh." Jessica made a face.

Elizabeth put her head back onto her pillow. She tried hard to think of another way that Eva could have escaped from their dreams. But her mind wouldn't focus. Again and again she saw the evil face of Eva Sullivan floating above her on the widow's walk. And over and over she had one terrifying thought:

If I dragged her into the waking world, then I'll have to . . . drag her out.

Ten

◇

"First a whole day of school," Steven muttered. "And now this!"

Groaning, he tugged on a rock half buried in the Riccolis' lawn. It didn't move. The wheelbarrow at his side was already full of rocks, though none of them were as big as the gray one in front of him. Steven tugged again. He could feel sweat trickling from every pore in his body.

"Only four o'clock in the afternoon," he grumbled. "And a whole 'nother flower bed to dig up!"

Wrinkling his nose, Steven grabbed a spade and attacked the soil around the rock. The rock was humongous, that was for sure. Way bigger than a volleyball.

Steven had been landscaping nearly every day during the last couple of weeks. The money was good, but the work was harder than he'd expected. For one thing, it involved muscles. Steven was beginning to realize that he didn't have as many as he'd thought.

And for another thing, landscaping involved skill. Like being able to tell daisies from dandelions. For some strange reason Steven had yet to figure out, people wanted daisies in their gardens and wanted dandelions out. Daisies were flowers, but dandelions, as Mrs. Riccoli had told him the other day, were weeds. Steven shook his head.

I mean, they're both yellow, he reasoned. *What's the big deal?*

In fact, as far as Steven could tell, the only difference between a weed and a flower was that weeds grew and flowers didn't. At least, everything he'd planted so far had died, while the things he hadn't planted had been growing all over the place.

Maybe he shouldn't have given those zinnias six bucketfuls of water at once. And as for those daisies he'd planted (or were they dandelions?), it seemed as if every time a bunch came up, it had mysteriously disappeared the next day.

No, they couldn't have been dandelions. Weeds wouldn't do that.

Oh, well. Wiping his forehead, he got on his knees and dug harder.

To get his mind off the work, Steven thought about how clever he'd been to get his sisters to tell him about their "monster." By now he had a complete picture of Eva Sullivan. "The teddy bear monster," he muttered. "How could my sisters be afraid of a ghost that drags a teddy bear around, for crying out loud?"

He'd also learned that Eva's bunny slipper had been pink. And that her nightgown had had some kind of flower on it. Daisies, maybe. Or dandelions. He'd forgotten which.

All from oh-so-casual questions. The girls had never suspected a thing. He grinned, savoring his victory. Too bad he hadn't been able to talk Joe into joining him.

The last bits of soil slipped away from the rock. Steven dropped the spade. Flexing his fingers, he stood up, bent his knees, and wrapped his hands around the stone. *Oof.* It might be as big as a volleyball, but it was at least five times heavier. He braced himself.

One. Two. Three!

"Oh, man!" Steven staggered backward under the weight of the rock in his hands. *Volleyball, nothing!* he thought, trying to catch his breath. This baby was five times heavier than a *bowling* ball. At least!

With a supreme effort he waddled to the wheelbarrow and dropped the boulder into it with a crash. *Phew!* Suddenly he felt twenty pounds lighter. Cracking his knuckles to see if he still had any feeling left in them, he ambled back to the hole.

And frowned. There was a scrap of—something—directly beneath the spot where the rock had been. Plastic of some kind? Steven grabbed it between thumb and forefinger. *Not plastic. Cloth, maybe?*

Well, there was only one way to find out. With a sudden jerk Steven pulled the scrap out of the dirt. It came out easily.

"Definitely cloth," he said aloud. *Dirty* cloth. It was about a foot long, he decided, and three inches wide. One edge was jagged, as if it had been torn violently from something else. Rubbing the scrap against his jeans, Steven cleaned one corner enough to see that it had once been white. He leaned closer. White with—something on it.

Gently Steven stroked the fabric. There were about a dozen little raised spots. Each one looked like it was made up of hundreds of tiny little stitches. What was the word for that? He frowned. *Em-em—*

Embroidery. That's it.

Steven licked his finger and wiped away another layer of dirt. The embroidered places were yellow, he saw, and they were definitely in the shape of a flower.

A flower—

Steven froze.

Somehow this fabric seemed very familiar.

Steven's gaze traveled quickly around the yard, searching for clues. A light breeze rustled the leaves on a tree near the porch, and in the corner by the fence Steven could see the remains of the overwatered zinnias. There was the row of bushes, thick and green except for the section that he'd accidentally ridden the lawn tractor through. There was the abandoned shack, paint peeling, leaning sadly to one side on one corner of the property. A butterfly zigzagged across the yard, a flash of orange against the green of the grass.

He stared down at the scrap of cloth in his hand.

Well, it probably wasn't worth spending any time on. With a sigh Steven let the flowered cloth drop to the ground.

"Doesn't matter, anyway," he told himself.

Groaning, he dropped to his knees to dig out the next rock.

"Here we are," Jessica said in a strangled voice. She stared nervously up into the sky, almost afraid to look in front of her. "The Sullivan family plot."

"It's big," Elizabeth said. Jessica could see her

sister trembling slightly in the gathering darkness. She could understand why. A cemetery wasn't the best place she could think of to spend an evening.

After school that day the twins had decided to pay a visit to Sweet Valley Meadows Cemetery, hoping to learn more about Eva Sullivan. But it had taken practically an hour to find the right section of the old graveyard, and now night was starting to fall.

Jessica shivered. She forced herself to look at the heavy iron rail that encircled the tombstones. A small tarnished plaque met her eyes. "Sacred to the memory of the Sullivan family," she read, straining to make out the words in the dim light.

Elizabeth hitched up her belt and shrugged halfheartedly. "Guess we might as well go in."

Or we could just forget the whole thing and go home, Jessica thought. But she didn't say it aloud. "I guess so," she replied. "You first."

Elizabeth rolled her eyes. "OK."

The girls walked through the entrance and stopped by a tall marble monument. The letters on it were old, Jessica saw, and in some places the wind and rain had worn the carving down to nearly nothing. "'Here lies Eva Sullivan,'" she read, a catch in her voice. She stared blankly at the grave in front of her. "Oh, man."

Elizabeth shook her head. "It's not our Eva," she said, pointing to the stone. "Keep reading."

" 'Beloved wife of—' " Jessica frowned, but her heart returned to normal. No way *their* Eva Sullivan had been anybody's wife. "I can't make that part out."

Elizabeth pointed to the bottom of the monument. "*This* Eva would have been one of *our* Eva's ancestors, I guess."

Jessica peered over her twin's shoulder to see. " 'Departed this earth June 17, 1834,' " she read. "I wonder how she died."

"Could have been anything," Elizabeth said softly. "People back then died of lots of things. They didn't have medicines like now. She might have gotten the measles or scarlet fever or something."

"Or maybe there was an accident," Jessica suggested. On the eastern horizon the stars were beginning to come out, twinkling in the fading brightness of the day. She took a deep breath. It was strange to see such a beautiful sky in such a spooky place as a cemetery.

"Or she could have died in childbirth," Elizabeth suggested. She took a step away from the grave. "Lots of women did back in those days."

First you have a child, and then you die. . . . A sudden chill swept over Jessica. She took a step back too and then another and another, stumbling over the iron rail in her hurry. "Let's find the grave we're looking for," she said with determination. "It's—it's not getting any lighter."

Elizabeth nodded soberly. "Let's," she agreed, fumbling for her sister's hand.

The back of the Sullivan plot was not well kept. Elizabeth noticed right away how rumpled the grass was. Even the ground itself seemed uneven and rocky.

"I—I think we must be close," Jessica said in a voice just barely above a whisper. "These must have been—her parents."

Elizabeth bent down to look at the two headstones side by side in the barren earth. The grave markers were made of shiny brown marble and reflected the moonlight off their smooth surfaces. "Thomas Sullivan," she read slowly, shading her eyes. "And Jane Sullivan." Her heart thudded in her chest. "Look at when they died," she murmured.

"I—I know." Jessica twisted her hands nervously. "Thomas died twenty years ago. And Jane . . ." Her voice trailed off.

"And Jane died just this summer," Elizabeth

supplied. She stared hard at the graves, willing them to reveal more information. "That must be when the mansion was sold to the Riccolis, Jess. And look." She ran her finger along the birth and death dates. "They weren't all that old either." *Thomas was forty-eight,* she figured. *And Jane was sixty-one—no, sixty.*

Jessica sucked in a long, shivering breath. "Let's get out of here, Lizzie. The moon's giving me a headache, and I thought I just heard a stick cracking in the woods." She motioned to the forest that lay just beyond the last row of graves, separated by a tall brick wall from the graveyard itself. "And it's *really* getting dark now."

Part of Elizabeth longed to leave too. But she knew she couldn't give up quite so easily. "There's one last grave back here," she said. "Let's take a quick look. Then we'll go."

"A quick look, that's all." Jessica set her jaw.

"Yeah." There was a faint scurrying sound somewhere off in the forest, but Elizabeth did her best to ignore it. She kept her eyes fixed on the single small gravestone ahead of her, feeling her way across the uneven ground with her feet.

"Look." Jessica tugged at Elizabeth's shirtsleeve. "Aren't those daisies?"

Elizabeth followed her sister's gaze.

Scattered on the bare ground in front of the small tombstone lay a pile of wilted daisies. "That's strange," Elizabeth mused, half to herself. Stooping, she picked up a flower and held it for a moment before letting it fall back to the earth. "This isn't like most of the bouquets here," she said slowly. "The stems aren't cut evenly, know what I mean?"

Jessica nodded. Her eyes looked troubled. "Yeah. These look like they've been—ripped out of the ground."

"Uh-huh." Elizabeth swallowed hard. "And the other bouquets were all arranged neatly. These—" She shook her head.

"Dumped," Jessica finished for her. "As if the person who put them here didn't bother to do it right."

"Or couldn't," Elizabeth added softly. *Couldn't risk being seen, maybe,* she thought.

Or didn't know how to do it properly . . .

"Let's get out of here." Jessica stared off into the sky, which was almost completely dark by now.

"Hold on," Elizabeth said, bending down. "I want to make sure it's her grave." There were words carved into the tombstone, small words, scarcely half an inch high. She wished she'd brought a flashlight. The moon had crept behind a cloud, so there wasn't enough light to see much of anything. Her pulse pounded through her temples as she strained to make out the name.

"Lizzie!" Jessica's voice sounded thin and faint. "But we *know*—"

"Hold *on!*" Elizabeth dropped even lower. The name began with an *E*, that much was sure. *E-V*—

No doubt about it. Elizabeth sat bolt upright. "It's Eva's tombstone, all right," she said, her words echoing across the Sullivan family plot. "And there're some other words too."

Slowly the cloud drifted off and unveiled the moon. Eva Sullivan's grave was bathed in a warm yellow glow. Jessica slid softly to her own knees beside her sister, the shadow of her head reflected onto the top of the tombstone. "Other words?" she asked curiously. "Like—what?"

"'Eva Sullivan, our darling daughter,'" Elizabeth read. For some reason a sudden chill ran up her spine.

"Our darling daughter," Jessica murmured beside her.

"Her parents must have loved her very much," Elizabeth said slowly, not sure whether that love made Eva's death more or less tragic. Her eyes flicked to the dates carved below Eva's name. "Oh, Jess, she was only eight when she died." *Eight years old—* She bit her lip. How terribly sad her parents must have been.

"And look," Jessica went on. She stabbed her finger at the tombstone. "October 31, Elizabeth. She died on Halloween!"

"Halloween," Elizabeth repeated. She shuddered. "Halloween, twenty-five years ago."

"When Mom was about our age," Jessica whispered.

Elizabeth nodded. Changing her position so the shadow of her own head wouldn't block her view, she read the last line on the marker aloud. "'May our daughter sleep at last in eternal peace.'"

The wind seemed to sigh above their heads. Another cloud raced forward and blotted out the moon. A pair of swallows darted like bats through the evening sky, skimming low in search of insects. The words seemed to echo in Elizabeth's mind. *May our daughter sleep at last . . .*

Jessica pulled up her collar. "I bet—" she began. She took a deep breath. "I bet Eva's not sleeping in peace."

"Or letting anyone else sleep in peace either," Elizabeth added grimly. She couldn't escape the feeling that the grave raised more questions than it answered.

"Can we go now?" Jessica pleaded.

Elizabeth nodded slowly.

But just then the moon came out from behind a cloud.

And Elizabeth turned in horror, a scream rising in her throat.

Because now there weren't just two shadows silhouetted against Eva Sullivan's tombstone—but three.

Eleven

"Run!" Jessica shouted. Her legs felt like jelly, but somehow she managed to get in gear. In an instant she had darted away from the grave with the daisies scattered on the top.

With a snarl Eva Sullivan lunged for the spot where Jessica had once been. But she tripped on the uneven ground and fell headlong to the earth with a terrible cry. The bunny slipper spun off her foot and came to rest by the tombstone.

Jessica barely noticed. She couldn't take her eyes off Eva. The figure on the ground looked even more horrible in the half darkness. *One leg twisted—fingers clawing at the earth—*

Steadying herself against the tombstone, Eva struggled to her feet. Jessica was amazed to see how small she was. With an inhuman wail the girl stumbled forward, arms outstretched.

Jessica turned and ran as fast as she could, her hair streaming away from her face. Ahead of her Elizabeth was already pounding toward the low iron rail that separated the Sullivan family plot from the rest of the cemetery. "Elizabeth!" Jessica shouted. "Wait up!"

Behind her the monster hissed. Jessica's hands felt sweaty, and her breath was coming in short gasps. She didn't dare look back to see if the monster was gaining.

"Elizabeth!" she shouted. "The railing!"

Instead of heading through the gate Elizabeth changed direction and leaped gracefully over the rail. Jessica followed a second later. *I hope Eva's too small to get across*, Jessica thought, panting as she ran.

Dashing behind a huge stone marker, Elizabeth turned to look behind her. "Which way?" she whispered breathlessly.

Which way? "Left?" Jessica said uncertainly, coming to a stop in the shadows next to her twin. The truth was, she had no idea where they should turn.

"I thought we had to go right," Elizabeth said. She stood perfectly still. "Can you hear her?"

Jessica hesitated. She strained to hear the monster—the footsteps, the hissing, the howls.

But all she could hear was the calls of a few birds somewhere in the distance.

"Do you think she's—" she began, hardly daring to wonder if they'd really escaped.

Elizabeth crouched down low to the ground. "This is a good hiding place, anyway," she whispered. "I'll look around and see if she's still there." Grabbing the edge of a tall stone tower, she began to shift her weight.

"Be careful!" Jessica whispered. Then she bit her lip, afraid that even whispering made too much noise.

"I will," Elizabeth assured her. Little by little she edged her head around the corner.

"Well?" Jessica couldn't stand the suspense. Nervously she cracked her knuckles, then stopped in alarm. *Don't make a sound*, she told herself sternly. *Not a sound!*

Elizabeth leaned a little farther.

"Can you see anything?" Jessica whispered, but her voice was so soft, Elizabeth didn't hear.

Jessica had never realized how hard it was to remain completely silent. There was a little tickle in the back of her throat, and she desperately needed to cough. To distract herself, she leaned gently against the monument and traced the letters carved onto the rough stone. *Samuel and Tamara Duke*. Jessica felt suddenly grateful to Mr. and Mrs. Duke for protecting them.

With an abrupt movement Elizabeth stood and turned to Jessica, her mouth a tight line. "She's *there*," she whispered.

"She's where?" Jessica asked, louder than she'd intended.

"There," Elizabeth mouthed back, gesturing toward the front of the monument.

Jessica's heart sank. "How far?" she mouthed, spreading out her hands to show different distances.

Elizabeth looked puzzled. "She's not a fish," she mouthed back. She held her own hand at chest level to show Jessica how tall Eva actually was.

Jessica felt a surge of irritation. "How *far*?" she mouthed again, exaggerating the movements of her lips. "How far away?"

Elizabeth's eyes widened with understanding. "Sorry," she mouthed. "Ten feet?" She held up all her fingers and pointed to the ground.

Ten feet. Great. Jessica wished her heart would stop beating so hard. Very gently she wiped sweat away from her forehead. *At least sweat doesn't make a noise.* Now that she thought about it, she could hear Eva's faint hissing sound from somewhere on the other side of the Dukes' monument.

Elizabeth gestured helplessly. "Should we run?" she mouthed, making running motions with her fingers.

Jessica bit her lip. She glanced around the rest of the cemetery. Darkness shrouded almost everything. The moon was behind a dense bank of clouds, and only a few dying rays of sunlight remained on the western rim of the sky. She shook her head. She couldn't imagine trying to run through the graveyard at night, even without a horrible monster chasing them. "Here," she mouthed, pointing hard at the ground. "Stay here!" She wanted to cough so badly. . . .

Elizabeth nodded and put out a hand to support herself against the monument.

Whatever was in Jessica's throat was beginning to feel like an elephant. She didn't know how much longer she could wait to cough. Was it her imagination, or was the hissing getting louder?

And were those tiny little footsteps?

Jessica couldn't help herself. Dropping to the ground, she peeked around the edge of the Dukes' monument. For a moment she could see nothing at all. Then as her eyes adjusted she could just make out the narrow road that led— one way or the other—to the entrance. Across the path were more headstones.

And on the path, walking slowly away, was a very familiar figure. Jessica had no trouble recognizing the small, lurching body of Eva Sullivan. *She's taking off,* she thought with relief. *She doesn't know where we are!*

Instantly the lump in Jessica's throat disappeared. She didn't have to cough after all. Her whole body began to relax.

But just at that moment the loudest sound Jessica had ever heard tore through her ears. It sounded like a pistol shot.

"Elizabeth!" Jessica turned and stared at her sister accusingly.

"I'm sorry!" Elizabeth whispered back. "But my throat was itching like crazy, and I just *had* to cough!"

On the narrow road the figure of Eva Sullivan paused suddenly, her bare feet planted firmly on the cement. Then slowly, like a hunting dog trained to find its prey, she turned.

And even in the darkness her half-dead eyes seemed to flash as her gaze met Jessica's.

"Run!" Jessica cried, nearly pushing her sister out of the way in her panic. Scarcely bothering to look where she was going, she ran off into the night, Elizabeth at her heels.

"I don't even know where we are," Elizabeth muttered as she and Jessica stopped running. Eva Sullivan seemed to have lost the track. *She may be strong, but at least she isn't fast*, Elizabeth told herself. Her head spun as she and her sister crept between enormous, looming headstones.

"I think—" Jessica broke off and licked her

lips. "I think we'd better stay on the road, don't you?"

Elizabeth considered. "That's where she'd probably be expecting us," she said. She resolved not to think about what would happen if Eva was waiting at the entrance gate. "I think we're better off if we stick to the outside," she went on. "If we follow the wall, then we're bound to find the entrance eventually."

Jessica nodded. "You're right," she said. "The road's like a maze, anyway. And if we stay near the wall—" She stopped short.

"What?" Elizabeth asked in a soft voice.

Jessica shivered. "Never mind," she said quickly.

But Elizabeth guessed what her sister was thinking. *If we stay near the wall, then we can climb over it in an emergency.*

"This way," she said, pointing.

Carefully the twins began to pick their way toward the brick wall at the back of the cemetery.

"This is so creepy," Jessica said in an unsteady voice. Keeping one hand firmly against the wall, she maneuvered toward what she hoped was the entrance.

"What's creepy?" Elizabeth asked.

Jessica made a face and motioned to the tidy rows of graves nearby. "When I think how all these people used to be alive, and now they're dead—" She shook her head. "It's just—spooky. Know what I mean?" She tried not to think of once-living human bodies decaying under-ground in their coffins, but it was no use. Every vampire movie she'd ever seen on TV seemed to be on reruns in her mind.

"But these people aren't after us," Elizabeth pointed out.

Jessica took a deep breath. "I know."

"And we don't know that Eva's a ghost," Elizabeth went on.

In the distance a twig snapped. Jessica froze, fighting a rising sense of panic. She wished she were anywhere except in this awful cemetery, playing hide-and-seek with a ghost who might not be a ghost, a girl who might not be a girl.

Gingerly Elizabeth stepped forward. "Look, don't you recognize this part of the graveyard?" she asked.

Jessica looked around her. Now that Elizabeth mentioned it, the section they were in did seem somehow familiar. There was a marble fountain to one side and a tall angel on a pedestal directly in front of them. "Yeah, I think so," she said softly. Was this place right at the entrance?

Elizabeth motioned toward a small tombstone surrounded by a stone wall. "I'm almost sure I remember that one," she said, smiling faintly at her sister. "Maybe we're on the right track."

Jessica cautiously stepped forward. The grave-yard seemed to be going on forever. The moon was there one minute, gone the next, giving the whole scene an even eerier feeling. She concentrated on the landmarks near her. *A statue . . . a tower with a sphere on the top . . .*

She blinked hard. If she remembered it so well, why did she have such a bad feeling about it?

Elizabeth stepped over a low iron rail and came to a stop in front of a tall marble monument. "This is *so* familiar," she murmured. A frown spread across her face.

Jessica looked around. She'd been here before, that was for sure—and she wished she hadn't. She thought she could hear footsteps resounding from behind every tombstone. Ghostly figures seemed to rise up everywhere she looked. "Let's get out of here," she urged.

"But—but—" Elizabeth spread out her hands helplessly. "Where *are* we?"

Jessica forced herself to think. Reaching forward, she stroked the smooth marble in front of her. And as she did a memory swept over her:

The twins stepping over a low iron rail and into the Sullivan family plot.

Where the first tombstone they saw was a tall marble monument.

The memory seemed a hundred years ago, but in her heart Jessica knew it was less than an hour old.

And then—no longer in her memory, but in real life—Jessica heard a hissing sound behind her. Turning quickly, she saw a sudden flash of white.

A nightgown was billowing in the wind.

"It's Eva!" she shrieked, pointing frantically toward the grave and pulling Elizabeth by the arm.

"Oh, man," Elizabeth moaned. She couldn't believe their awful luck. Somehow in the darkness they'd gotten completely turned around. Somehow they'd ignored clues that they were going back to the Sullivan plot. And now they would pay for it.

Her heart hammering in her chest, Elizabeth backed around the tombstones, praying that she'd somehow manage to find a weapon. *A tree branch—a stone—* Her mind whirled.

In front of them Eva Sullivan walked forward with a steady, merciless gait. Her scarred face reflected the glow of the moon back to the girls. Somewhere deep in her throat Eva made a low growling sound.

"No!" Elizabeth begged. Her voice caught.

"Please!" Jessica added.

The creature came forward, her eyes gleaming.

Out of the corner of her eye Elizabeth could see the graves of Thomas and Jane Sullivan. The ground beneath her feet was bare and uneven. They must be almost on top of Eva's own grave. She shivered. Her ankle brushed against something small and furry. For an instant Elizabeth froze. Then she relaxed.

The bunny slipper, she told herself, remembering how it had flown off Eva's foot when she had attacked them earlier. The tombstone shielded the slipper from Eva's sight. Bending down, Elizabeth grabbed the slipper and thrust it into her pocket. *You never know,* she thought. *It might come in handy.*

"We have to climb the wall," Jessica hissed in the silence.

Elizabeth clenched and unclenched her fists. Jessica was right, she realized. The creature was steadily backing them against the wall. "Do you think—" she began, then stopped, afraid to say the rest. The wall looked awfully high.

"We have to." Jessica's voice was steely hard in the darkness.

Eva grunted and licked what was left of her lips. Her clawlike fingers flexed. Elizabeth felt suddenly faint.

"Turn and run," Jessica whispered. "I'll boost you. Then you pull me up."

Every muscle in Elizabeth's body felt weak. Desperately she tried not to look at Eva.

"One—two—" Jessica said softly. "Three! Run!"

Together the twins turned and ran to the edge of the cemetery. At the base of the wall Jessica cupped her hands. "Now!" she hissed.

Heart thumping, Elizabeth stepped into her sister's interlaced fingers.

"Hurry!" Jessica winced as she boosted her sister. Elizabeth held her breath, trying to make herself as light as possible. Her fingers scrabbled against the bricks.

"I said hurry!" Jessica said urgently.

"I'm trying!" Elizabeth grabbed the top of the wall with her left hand and tried to pull herself up. Her bare elbow dug into the rough concrete, but Elizabeth scarcely noticed. With her knee she pushed against the bricks. *I can do it—I can do it—* she thought frantically, hoping against hope that she actually could. Slowly but surely her feet lifted off Jessica's hands.

"Hurry!" Jessica shrieked.

"I'm almost there!" Elizabeth's chest was now even with the edge of the wall. She hooked both hands over the top and strained every muscle she had. With her last ounce of energy she swung her legs onto the wall and lay there, panting.

"But—Eliz—!" The word caught in Jessica's throat.

Elizabeth stared down in alarm. Eva Sullivan was closing in fast.

Elizabeth knew she had to act. Wrapping her legs and her left arm firmly around the top of the wall, she stretched her right hand down to her sister. "Grab hold!" she shouted.

"I—I can't!" Jessica jumped, but her fingers barely brushed Elizabeth's.

Elizabeth leaned farther, as far as she dared. "Try again," she commanded, her eyes locking with Jessica's.

Jessica jumped again. This time her fingertips touched Elizabeth's palm. Elizabeth strained to close her hand over her sister's, but she was too late.

"Help!" Jessica's eyes widened in terror.

Elizabeth knew she had no choice. Letting go with her left hand, she stretched her body so her head was pointing almost directly down. Concrete bit into her legs, but she refused to think about the pain. With her right hand she groped in her pocket for the slipper she'd grabbed from Eva's grave. She'd just have to hope she could keep her balance.

The hissing sound was louder than ever.

Elizabeth gripped the slipper with all her strength and dangled her entire body over the side. "Now!" she cried out. "Come on, Jess, jump!"

Jessica leaped. In the next split second Elizabeth could see Eva lunging toward the spot where her sister had just stood. Jessica's body arched upward. She reached out her hand.

Elizabeth braced herself. Suddenly the full weight of Jessica's body was pulling her down, though she couldn't feel her sister's hand anywhere. She struggled to hold on. Her legs wrapped more tightly around the top of the wall, and Elizabeth tugged upward as hard as she could, careful not to let go of the bunny slipper for even a second.

Little by little Jessica came over the edge.

"That w-was . . . so close," Jessica stammered, swinging her legs up over the wall. Below them Eva snarled, and her eyes flashed angrily. "I thought I wouldn't make it—but where'd you get the slipper from?"

"No time to talk now." Elizabeth patted Jessica's shoulder, oddly grateful to Eva for dropping the slipper. Without it she could never have reached far enough to grab her sister's hand. "Let's get out of here!" Still holding the slipper, she dropped over the wall and into the forest.

It was still dark, and it was still a long way home.

But at least, she thought as she and Jessica started running through the trees, *we're on the right side of the wall!*

Twelve

Elizabeth opened her eyes and checked her alarm clock. *Five-thirty.* She yawned and rolled over. *Way* too early to get up for school. She shut her eyes and tried to go back to sleep.

But the more she tried, the more wakeful she felt. There was a gnawing feeling in the pit of her stomach, a feeling that just plain wouldn't go away.

It's Halloween, she thought bleakly.

Elizabeth sighed. Most Halloweens she'd wake as early as possible and cruise through the day until it was time for trick-or-treating.

But somehow this Halloween was different.

The trouble is, no place is safe anymore, Elizabeth thought. The monster could show up anywhere, she realized. At the Riccolis', at home, in the graveyard. Elizabeth shuddered, remembering that this was the anniversary of the day when Eva Sullivan had died.

Could she come to school? she wondered. In her mind's eye she saw Eva walking into her homeroom, hissing and swaying from side to side. She saw Eva reaching sharp twisted claws toward her. Eva pushing her savagely against the chalkboard. Eva finishing what she'd started on the roof the other night.

Elizabeth drew a deep breath.

There's nowhere to hide, she thought miserably.

Rolling over again, she struggled to fill her mind with peaceful images. *Flowers,* she thought. A picture of a field of daisies popped into her mind.

Then her stomach knotted. She still saw the daisies, only not in the field. Now they were scattered over Eva Sullivan's grave.

No! she thought emphatically, squeezing her eyes tightly closed. Songbirds were calling outside her window. She concentrated on their twittering. *Birds are nice,* she thought. In her mind she could almost see them—their crested heads, their soft feathers, their long claws.

Their claws. Elizabeth sat bolt upright as she pictured Eva's clawlike fingernails.

"I guess—I guess I'll stay awake," she murmured. Sitting up, she turned on the light and grabbed the book that lay on her bedside table. She opened it up and tried to locate her favorite passages. But she couldn't absorb a single word.

She was thinking about something else. Something much more alarming than what was going on in *Persuasion.*

Today is the day, she told herself, her fingers nervously beating on the edge of the paperback.

Something horrible—something terrifying—is going to happen today.

Jessica slammed her locker shut and grabbed her book bag. *Three o'clock,* she thought grimly. School was over, but she was afraid trouble was just beginning.

"Ready to roll, Lizzie?" she asked her twin, her mouth a tight line.

"I—I guess so." Elizabeth shook her head tiredly. "What time are we due at the Riccolis', anyway?"

"Nine o'clock," Jessica answered. "Plenty of time for trick-or-treating before we go over. That'll be good, huh?" She plastered her biggest, phoniest grin on her face, wishing they could cancel the baby-sitting job. Wishing they could cancel trick-or-treating.

Wishing they could cancel Halloween altogether.

"I was just thinking," Elizabeth said briskly.

"Maybe we need backup tonight. Like, reinforcements?" Her eyes darted nervously up and down the corridor. "It's not that I think anything's going to happen," she continued with a little laugh. "It's just that, you know, five Riccoli kids on Halloween night are going to be kind of a handful."

Jessica grinned faintly. "You're right," she said, craning her neck. "So we should find Todd and Amy and Winston and see if they're free tonight." She coughed. "I mean, tell them they need to help us out at nine tonight."

"Sounds good," Elizabeth agreed. "Hey, do you think they've seen . . . you know . . ." She paused.

Eva, Jessica filled in, but she didn't want to say the name aloud. "I don't know," she said. Her mouth felt suddenly dry. "Probably not," she said, trying to shrug carelessly. "I mean, they'd have told us, right?"

"I guess so." Elizabeth scratched her chin. "But we didn't tell—I mean—" She looked at the ground and shook her head.

"We'll tell them what's happened," Jessica agreed. "Then—"

"Hey, Jessica!" Startled, Jessica whirled around. Lila stood grinning behind her.

"There's Amy," Elizabeth whispered in Jessica's ear. "I'll grab her before she leaves." She scurried down the hallway.

"I haven't seen you around, Jessica," Lila said. "I wanted to talk to you about—" She paused dramatically.

"About what, Lila?" Jessica asked, edging toward her locker.

Lila dropped her voice to a conspiratorial whisper. "About *tonight*. You're not still planning to *baby-sit*, are you?" she asked, rolling her eyes to show what she thought of the idea.

With all her heart, Jessica wished she weren't. "Um—yeah," she admitted. "But not until nine o'clock."

"Nine o'clock." Lila's voice was full of scorn. "Please, Jessica! Get real! You'll miss trick-or-treating. And the party of the century." She fixed Jessica with a look. "Are you *sure* you can't come? It won't be the same without you."

"Um—" Jessica began. She was feeling sorry for herself all over again.

"I mean, I'll have to listen to Janet Howell talk about *her* costume all night long," Lila interrupted. "My costumes are always better than hers, but the way she talks about hers, well—" She frowned. "And your costumes are always so—interesting, Jessica. They're not very fancy, but they sure are sensible. Next to you I always look so—um—I mean—"

Jessica folded her arms across her chest. She suspected that Lila was making fun of her.

"What are you going as this year, anyway?" Lila asked.

"Um—Marilyn Monroe," Jessica said.

"Marilyn Monroe," Lila repeated blankly. "Hmmm . . . maybe you'd better not come with us at all, Jessica."

"Why not?" Jessica frowned.

"Oh, nothing." Lila raised one hand in the air and slowly let it drop. "Just that a whole bunch of *fourth-graders* are going as Marilyn Monroe, that's all. Grace and Kimberly were going to buy that same costume. Until they discovered how totally juvenile it was."

Fourth-graders. Good grief. Jessica felt like kicking herself. Bad enough to have to baby-sit at a haunted house. But dressing in the same costume as little kids was much worse.

"Well, *Marilyn*, we're meeting at Casey's at eight-thirty," Lila said. She wiggled her fingers at Jessica. "Be there or be square!"

Jessica took a deep breath and looked at the floor.

Be there or be square?

Did she have a choice?

Steven groaned. *Four o'clock on Halloween,* he thought frantically, *and I haven't even finished my costume yet!*

He surveyed the table in front of him. For a

nightgown Steven had decided to use a white bedsheet. To make it look old and worn, he'd dragged it through the dirt over at the Riccolis' house. But he'd only just begun putting on the dandelions or whatever they were. He hoped yellow permanent marker would show up in the dark. The trouble was, he'd been so busy getting the makeup just right, everything else had been shoved to the back burner.

Of course, he reflected proudly, the makeup was way, *way* cool. Steven stared at himself in the mirror. The scars, long and angry and deep across the cheeks. The hair streaked with gray and white. The blacked-out teeth, the hint of a cheekbone sticking up out of the putrid flesh, the clawlike fingernails. All just the way the twins had described.

He narrowed his eyes and put on the most ghastly face he could. *Yup. Perfect.*

But he still had to try walking with the "nightgown" on. Standing up, Steven pinned the old piece of cloth over his shoulders. He'd cut holes for the arms already. Adjusting the nightgown so it hung straight down, he clumped across the room in the uneven way that his sisters had told him the monster walked. *Not bad, not bad.* He did it again, exaggerating the limp even more. *Better. Definitely better.*

Steven's fingers absentmindedly stroked the

sheet, moving it a little off his hip. He looked down, and he caught a flash of yellow. For a moment he stood perfectly still, remembering.

Remembering another piece of cloth with yellow flowers on it.

Buried under a rock, somewhere in the Riccolis' garden.

Steven knitted his brows. *Of course it's only a coincidence*, he told himself. *Who says that scrap was from a nightgown?*

And who says it ever belonged to someone who lived in that house? And who says that Eva Whatever-her-name-is lived there to begin with?

"Just a coincidence." Steven chuckled.

But his throat felt suddenly dry.

And for the briefest of instants he had the sneaking suspicion that maybe this costume wasn't such a great idea.

"Well, I'm glad the others can help us out tonight," Elizabeth said softly as the twins headed for home. They'd gone over to Winston's after school, where they'd talked about what had happened in the graveyard and how Eva had appeared at the Wakefields' house.

Unfortunately, Elizabeth thought gloomily, the other kids hadn't come up with any answers.

Lots of questions. But no answers.

"Yeah." Jessica jammed her hands into her

pockets. "I guess it was a good sign that none of them had seen anything weird," she said. "Wasn't it?"

Elizabeth nodded. "Probably it means we're the only crazy ones," she said, forcing out a little chuckle. Actually she had felt just a tiny bit jealous of the other kids. None of them had seen Eva since the day Mrs. Riccoli had come home from Florida. "Time to put on our costumes," she said, changing the subject.

"Yeah," Jessica said heavily.

They walked on in silence.

Teddy bear. Teddy bear. Teddy bear!

Steven could hardly believe he'd forgotten to get a teddy bear. It had been years since he'd had one himself, and there was no possible way he was going out to the mall dressed like this to buy a new one. Besides which, he was flat broke. He racked his brain. Could he do without it? he wondered.

No—probably not. The twins were always talking about—

"The twins!" he murmured, smacking his fist into his palm. His eyes lit up. "That's it!"

Hadn't Jessica said that she'd grabbed the bear away from the monster? And hadn't she said it was in her closet?

There was only one thing to do. Gently Steven

pushed open the door of his room. "Hello?" he called out experimentally. He didn't think anyone was home, but he figured he should be safe.

No answer.

Steven eased his door all the way open. With his eyes he measured the distance to Jessica's room. For no obvious reason, his heart was pounding furiously. *There's nobody in the house, Wakefield*, he told himself sternly. *Just do it!*

Steven took a deep breath. Then, grabbing the ends of the sheet so he wouldn't trip, he sailed into Jessica's room.

He only hoped the closet wouldn't be a total mess.

"Maybe—" Jessica began. Turning the corner, the twins walked slowly down Calico Drive toward their house.

Elizabeth raised her eyebrows. "Maybe what?" she asked.

"Oh—nothing." Jessica sighed for what seemed like the eighth time today. "I'm hoping we'll have a message when we get home, that's all."

"A message?" Elizabeth repeated.

Jessica shrugged halfheartedly. What was the use in even thinking about it? She led the way up the porch steps. "A message on the answering machine," she explained in a tired voice. "You know, from Mr. and Mrs. Riccoli. Telling us that we don't have to come tonight. That one of the kids is sick or something." Not that she hoped one of the kids was. Not really. Still—

"Hey, yeah." Elizabeth looked at her sister and narrowed her eyes. "You don't suppose—"

But Jessica cut her off. "I doubt it," she said, shaking her head.

And anyway, she thought, *Eva will probably get us no matter where we are.*

"Hello?"

Buried deep inside the federal disaster area that was Jessica's closet, Steven felt his stomach slide suddenly sideways. Someone was home!

Please just don't come upstairs, he prayed silently. With one hand he swept a clay sculpture back onto a shelf. With the other he grabbed at the bear, which he'd found tucked under three pairs of shoes and a kilt that looked about six sizes too big for his sister. He took a step back, trying not to knock over a pile of videotapes. *Jessica would have a conniption if I—*

Wait a minute. Steven stared down. What was that on the floor? Bending over, he picked up something pink and fuzzy. Something with a threadbare bunny face on one end.

"The bunny slipper!" Steven said softly. He kicked himself for his stupidity. Another thing he'd forgotten. Well, wherever it had come from, he'd take it too.

Footsteps sounded on the stairs.

Oh, man! It was probably Jessica, Steven thought. It would be just his luck. She'd come in and then all his preparations would be totally spoiled. His brain whirled. Back into the closet? *No. She might find me and then what?*

He had to make a run for it. Taking a deep breath, Steven barreled across Jessica's room, out the door, and into the hall. His heart raced. Dashing into his own bedroom, he came to a skittering stop and locked the door firmly behind him.

He was just catching his breath when he heard someone scream.

"Elizabeth! Come quick!"

Elizabeth took the steps two at a time, her heart pounding in her chest. She had never heard Jessica sound so frantic. "What is it?" she yelled.

Jessica leaned against the railing, her fingers pointing toward Steven's door. "Eva!" she cried, squeezing her eyes shut tight as if to make the image go away. "She's here in this house!"

Elizabeth stared at her sister, then at the closed door that led into her brother's room. "In Steven's room?" she asked in disbelief.

"Yes!" Jessica covered her face with her hands.

"I knew she'd get us, Lizzie, I *knew* she would!" She stepped backward and nearly fell down the stairs.

"Calm down, calm down," Elizabeth soothed her sister. She cast an anxious look at the door. Things seemed pretty quiet behind it, but how could you tell for sure? "What did you see, Jess? Tell me exactly."

"I was coming up to put my book bag in my closet," Jessica gasped out between sobs. "And Eva was right in the hall! Then she went into Steven's room and slammed the door."

Elizabeth frowned. Something was strange here. "Usually the monster tries to attack us," she said. "Why would she—"

"I *know!*" Jessica stared Elizabeth in the face. "But it was *her!*" she insisted. Tears welled in her eyes. "She looked bigger than normal, but she was in that nightgown, and she had a teddy bear, and the face looked like hers, and everything!"

Elizabeth came to a quick decision. Taking Jessica's hand, she dragged her sister up to the second floor. "We're going to find out what's going on," she said in her bravest voice.

Jessica's only answer was a sob.

"Steven?" Elizabeth rapped on the door with her knuckles. "Are you home?"

A tired voice came from inside the room.

"Huh? Whazzat?" It was followed by a strange-sounding snore.

"That's Steven, all right," Elizabeth hissed to Jessica. She tried the handle, but it wouldn't move. "May we come in? It's important."

"Huh?" Steven sounded even sleepier than before. He yawned loudly. "No—sorry—I, uh."

"You're what?" Elizabeth rattled the handle again.

"Maybe he's being held hostage," Jessica whispered.

"I'm asleep," Steven said, yawning again.

Elizabeth sighed loudly. *Brothers!* "Listen, Steven. Is anybody in there with you?" she yelled through the keyhole.

"Huh? Whaddaya talking about?" Steven snapped. "I mean—no," he added in the same sleepy voice. "Just"—yawn—"me."

Elizabeth was amazed that one person could yawn so often in so little time. "Did anybody come *through* your room?"

"Go 'way." Steven yawned yet again. "Leave me—alone."

"There." Elizabeth turned back to Jessica. "Nothing to worry about. And it couldn't have been Eva because Eva doesn't have the teddy bear anymore, remember?"

Jessica cried even louder. "Then it's getting worse and worse," she sobbed.

"Worse and worse?" Elizabeth repeated blankly. "What do you mean?"

Jessica's eyes filled with fresh tears, and she buried her face in Elizabeth's sweater.

"Now I'm seeing her even when she isn't there!"

Thirteen

"Whoa, baby!" Andrew Riccoli shouted, shaking his fists in the air as he studied the pile of candy in front of him. "What a haul, huh?"

"I got more than you did," Gretchen announced, sticking out her tongue.

"Did not." Andrew frowned and looked enviously at his sister's candy. "If you took one of mine—" he threatened, snaking out an arm toward her pile.

"Mom!" Gretchen yelled very loudly.

"Come on, kids," Elizabeth pleaded. It was almost nine, and she and Jessica had just arrived at the Riccoli house. The other baby-sitters would be arriving any minute now. She threw a desperate look toward her sister. The evening was going to be hard enough, she thought. And if the kids were going to spend the rest of the night squabbling—

"Andrew and Gretchen!" Mrs. Riccoli, dressed in a ten-gallon hat and a shiny set of spurs, appeared in the doorway. "One more word and you're going straight to bed—no more candy, no more anything," she told them, waving her forefinger at them.

"Heh, heh," Andrew said uncertainly. "Just kidding."

"Yeah, same here," Gretchen put in, flashing a completely unconvincing grin at her brother. "Just a joke."

Mrs. Riccoli winked at Elizabeth. "I guess I shouldn't be too hard on them," she said. "After all, it *is* Halloween. And you're never too old to enjoy Halloween!"

"Are your parents dressing up tonight?" Mr. Riccoli asked the twins. He carried a rope around his shoulder, and he wore genuine cowboy boots just as he had promised he would. He looked from Elizabeth to Jessica and back. "Or should I say, Jane and Marilyn?"

Elizabeth blinked at him, surprised. Mr. Riccoli was the first person all evening who had guessed her costume. "How did you know I was—"

"I'm just an amazing guy," Mr. Riccoli replied, tapping his forehead and nodding knowingly.

Mrs. Riccoli leaned forward. "I told him," she stage-whispered.

Elizabeth giggled.

"Don't believe her," Mr. Riccoli said with a careless wave of his hand. "So are your folks wearing costumes?"

"Not this year," Jessica said, turning slightly pink.

"Too bad," Mr. Riccoli said. "I thought everyone liked Halloween. I know I'd hate to miss out on all the fun." He took his wife's arm. "Well, hold down the fort, now," he said in a singsong cowboy voice. "We'll be home before the cattle go to bed, OK?"

"But not before the children do," Mrs. Riccoli added dryly.

Elizabeth's heart did flip-flops as she watched Mr. and Mrs. Riccoli walk arm in arm toward the door. *They're leaving,* she thought, struggling to stay in control of herself.

And they're leaving us with the monster.

Something tugged at Elizabeth's skirt. Her chest tightening, she turned quickly. But instead of the twisted arm she half expected to see, there was only Nate, still dressed as a ghost.

She took a deep breath.

If every little sound makes me nervous, she thought, feeling her heart pumping at a mile a minute, *it's going to be a long, long night!*

*   *   *

"Aaaaah!"

Steven stood on the sidewalk, laughing uproariously. *Like shooting fish in a barrel,* he thought as he watched a goblin and a robot dashing down the block as fast as their legs could carry them. *One look at my pretty face—that's all it takes!*

It was all so incredibly easy. Patting his backpack, he retreated from the glare of the streetlight above his head. Right now he was dressed in an oversize black shirt and dark pants. He checked his watch. *Another ten minutes or so. Then I'll go change clothes and find my sisters.*

Heh, heh, heh.

Steven leaned innocently against a bush. The idea, he'd decided, was to stay as still as possible. When a trick-or-treater came by, he'd lunge forward, writhing and moaning and clawing frantically at the air. Nearly everyone screamed and ran. A few even dropped their bags of candy.

Footsteps sounded down the street. Steven looked around quickly. A tramp and a fairy princess. He squinted to make sure both figures were over four feet tall. Steven wasn't interested in scaring little kids. *Like I always say*, he reminded himself, *you've got to draw the line somewhere.*

The footsteps came nearer. Steven stood as

stiff and straight as possible. *Three—two—one—
Now!*

With a scream that practically scared himself,
Steven burst forward, sharp claws lunging toward the fairy princess.

"Aaaaah!" the trick-or-treaters screeched.

And in less than two seconds they were bolt-
ing down the block and into the night.

"One last candy, and then it's bedtime,"
Jessica announced. The hands of the grandfather
clock had never moved so slowly. She'd already
locked every window in the house, just in case.
Not that she thought it would do any good
against Eva.

Olivia flashed Jessica a sweet smile. "Can't I
have two? Please?"

"They're small," Andrew pointed out, looking
at Jessica eagerly.

"Just one," Jessica repeated firmly. She wasn't
in the mood to argue. *If I survive tonight,* she
thought with a growing sense of doom, *I am
never, ever coming back to this house again. And I
mean it this time.*

The doorbell rang. Jessica jumped.

"I'll get it!" Olivia made a dash for the front
door.

"Stop!" Jessica was on her feet before Olivia
had reached the hallway. Her voice echoed

throughout the living room. To her surprise, Jessica discovered that her hands were trembling.

"What's wrong?" Olivia spun quickly around.

It's probably the other baby-sitters, Jessica told herself. *And if it isn't, then it's just some late trick-or-treaters.*

Jessica tried her best not to think about the third possibility.

"What's wrong?" Olivia repeated, frowning.

Jessica plastered a smile on her face. "Nothing," she replied quickly. "Just ask who it is before you open the door."

Olivia gave Jessica a strange look. "Well, OK. But it *is* Halloween, you know."

Exactly, Jessica thought with dread as she sat back down on the couch.

Juliana sat down in Jessica's lap. "This is my last gumdrop," she said, reaching into her bag. "Do you want it?"

Jessica hugged the little girl. "No, thanks," she murmured. She wasn't feeling very hungry. "You eat it."

"OK." Juliana popped the gumdrop in her mouth. "You sound so sad," she remarked, chewing carefully. "Don't you like Halloween?"

There was a noise in the hallway, and Winston came in, dressed as a skeleton with a fake arrow sticking through his skull. Behind him came Amy, in a white coat and stethoscope, and Todd, dressed as Cal Ripken, complete with Baltimore Orioles cap and baseball bat. Jessica smiled faintly. *See?* she told herself. *There's nothing at all to be afraid of.*

Nothing. Nothing at all.

"Don't you like Halloween?" Juliana asked again, taking Jessica's hand in her own.

Jessica hesitated, choosing her words carefully. "I used to," she answered at last. "But I'm not sure I like it so much anymore."

Ducking out of sight behind a tree, Steven unzipped his backpack and grabbed his Eva Sullivan costume. First the nightgown. Careful not to disturb the makeup, he pulled it gently over his head. Even in the faint glow of the streetlight he could make out the yellow flowers. *Excellent.*

Next the bunny slipper. Steven was pretty sure his sisters had said that there was only one slipper. Just as well, since one was all he had. It was too small for his foot, but he decided to wear it, anyway. *I don't have to run*, he told himself, grinning evilly in the darkness. *And who cares if the slipper hurts? It'll just help me limp.*

He tugged on the slipper until his foot was in. It was hard with claws on. Oddly the back of the slipper was already covered with little cuts and scrapes. Almost as if it had been nicked many times by something sharp.

Steven frowned at the slipper. It was also funny how . . . how *old* it felt. As if it had gotten a lot of use years ago. Briefly he wondered again where his sisters had gotten it. But then he shrugged. What difference did it make?

Chuckling, Steven picked up the teddy bear. It was kind of old too, he noticed. He held it in different positions. *Facing out? Or facing in?* He decided that facing out looked better. The top of the head was almost completely threadbare, and one eye gazed vacantly from the bear's face. In a few places stuffing poked through the cloth.

Steven set the bear down for a moment to zip the backpack up. As he did he noticed a tag on the side of the bear. He picked it up again.

"Property of Eva Sullivan," he read, frowning. *Hmmm. That's strange.*

He'd sort of suspected that the bear was really Jessica's and the twins were making up the whole story about Eva Sullivan. But if the bear really belonged to Eva Sullivan, then—

But who says Eva Sullivan ever lived in that house, anyway? he asked himself. *Maybe the bear really did belong to someone named Eva Sullivan—but she was some kid who sold it to them at a garage sale or something.*

He nodded slowly. *Yeah. That makes sense.*

Still, it was kind of eerie.

Clutching the bear tightly to his chest, Steven limped off into the night in search of his sisters.

Somebody say something, Elizabeth thought, watching the flickering candles in the Riccolis' living room throw eerie shadows on the wall. *Somebody say something!*

But no one did.

Elizabeth imagined every entrance in the house. They had all been locked, hadn't they? The kids were all in bed. By now she hoped they were sound asleep. Nearby, huddled around the coffee table, were the other four baby-sitters.

Did anybody lock the back door? she thought suddenly, sitting up straight.

Jessica stared at her, her face frozen in an expression of terror. Winston jumped. Amy's fists clenched, while Todd's grip tightened on his baseball bat.

"What is it?" Jessica asked in a voice that wasn't quite her own.

"I—I was just wondering," Elizabeth said slowly. "Did anybody lock the back door?"

Amy nodded. "I did," she said. "Don't worry."

Elizabeth took a deep breath. "The basement window?"

"I took care of that one," Todd assured her.

"We checked 'em all," Winston said gruffly.

"Never fear. This house is *sealed*. Those kids can't get out."

Elizabeth swallowed hard. She wished that the kids' getting out was all she was afraid of.

The room was so silent, Elizabeth could hear herself breathe. In front of her a candle flickered, and in its faint light Elizabeth almost thought she saw Eva Sullivan hovering against the wall. She suppressed a gasp as a horrible thought formed in her mind.

They had locked up every entrance to the house that they knew about. . . . But what if there were other ways to get in and out? Entrances that Eva Sullivan—whoever she was—could use?

Entrances that the baby-sitters didn't know about. Entrances that they couldn't even see . . .

Steven limped down a dark alley not far from his house, seething with anger at his sisters. He'd taken all this time and trouble to dress up as their worst nightmare, and now what? The twins weren't anywhere to be found.

Not only that, people kept laughing at him. And no wonder. The nightgown was totally dorky. And what kind of a loser carried a teddy bear? At least no one had recognized him under all that makeup.

He hoped not, anyway.

And the bunny slipper was way too small.

"Way, *way* too small," Steven muttered. He should have taken it off half an hour ago. He'd probably have blisters on top of blisters tomorrow morning.

A small figure dressed in white was standing at the end of the alley. For a brief moment he hoped it was one of his sisters. But as he limped toward it he saw it was far too small to be the twins.

And too small for me to scare, he realized with disgust.

The figure began to move forward, lurching from side to side just as Steven was doing. There was a faint hissing sound.

Steven stopped in his tracks. For some reason his palms were suddenly sweaty.

The figure moved slowly but steadily in the same weird rocking motion. A shiver of fear crept along Steven's spine. Even in the darkness he could tell that the figure was wearing a nightgown.

A white nightgown. With little yellow flowers. With a place along the bottom where a jagged swatch of fabric had been ripped out. A swatch about a foot long and three inches wide.

"Hello?" Steven's voice cracked. He took a step back.

The figure reached out an arm. Steven gasped. In the faint light of the alley he could see something sharp glittering at the end of the hand. *A claw.* "No," he whispered, not daring to take his eyes off the creature in front of him. "It can't be."

But it was.

This isn't a costume, Steven thought, panicking as the creature came even nearer.

It was as though he was looking into a mirror. Every scar on his own face, every spot of discolored flesh was on the face in front of him too. Though he towered over the figure, he was terrified. The hissing sound grew louder.

"Get away from me!" Steven commanded, his voice sounding high and thin in the darkness. He groped for a weapon, but there was none. "I said get away!" Backing up again, he noticed that the figure was barefoot. Instinctively he looked down at his own feet, at the tiny bunny slipper, which—

Which, he realized, with a sinking heart, would be a perfect fit on the monster's own foot.

Wavering unsteadily, the monster stared Steven directly in the eye. Little flecks of foam stood out on her lips. Again her claws reached out, and her mouth opened a crack, revealing uneven, broken teeth.

"Give me—my bear."

The words were slurred, but Steven had no trouble understanding. His arm seemed frozen to his side.

"Give me my—*bear!*" The sound seemed to come straight out of the monster's throat. Its—her—torn and bruised lips barely moved.

"I—I—" Steven's cheek felt like a block of wood.

The monster lunged.

And the next thing Steven knew, he was lying flat on his back, gaping in horror as the beast's sharp claws descended rapidly toward his throat.

Fourteen

The doorbell rang.

Alone in her house, Mrs. Wakefield made no move to answer it. She sat in the darkened kitchen, her head in her hands, wishing the trick-or-treaters would go away. Wishing that she had never heard of Halloween.

She was glad she was alone, glad the kids were out, glad her husband was working late. Every Halloween was the same. Every Halloween since . . . since *it* had happened, so many years ago.

She took a deep breath. *I will not think about it*, a small voice inside her head insisted. *I will not!*

"Trick or treat?" someone asked outside the door.

Tensing all her muscles, Mrs. Wakefield stared at the wall.

The doorbell rang again. The sound stabbed deep into her heart, like a crystal-clear icicle. *No one is home!* she thought fiercely. She jerked her clenched fist to the side, disturbing the pile of mail that someone had stacked neatly on the table's edge.

She could hear muffled voices outside. Then after a moment Mrs. Wakefield heard the faint noise of footsteps walking away from the dark house.

She breathed deeply. *Safe.*

Mrs. Wakefield reached out to straighten the stack of mail. She glanced at the envelope on top—and her hand froze.

"To Mrs. Alice Wakefeeld," Mrs. Wakefield read in the dim light of the room. The large looping letters of a child just learning to write in cursive were somehow strangely familiar. A chill ran up her spine.

Her eyes searched for a return address, for some hint of the sender's identity. But the envelope was plain and blank except for the stamp and the scrawled address.

Mrs. Wakefield ripped open the envelope and lifted out a single sheet of paper. It was ordinary loose-leaf paper, badly smudged with ink. Someone had folded it many times, till it was almost as thick as it was wide.

There was something else in the envelope too. A photograph. With a feeling of dread Mrs. Wakefield probed the envelope and pulled it out. Steeling herself, she looked at it—

And screamed.

She had seen the picture before. But not for twenty-five years. And not like this. Never like this.

There, in the picture, was twelve-year-old Alice Wakefield leaning against a wall, grinning happily into the camera.

Her arm was wrapped around a younger girl, whose expression was pensive. Almost sad.

And at the bottom of the photo the words *Alice and Eva* were written in humpbacked childish letters.

The room seemed to spin. Her hand trembling, Mrs. Wakefield stared at the photo.

It didn't make sense.

Tears stung her eyes. None of it made sense.

And what made the least sense of all was the large black X that someone had drawn boldly across Eva's face—

And her own.

"Get away from me!" Steven hollered at the top of his lungs. Desperately he lifted his arm to ward off the claws. "Help!"

Hissing, the monster knocked aside Steven's

arm as if it were made of paper. "Help!" Steven shouted again, watching in terror as the claws groped for his neck. He hunched his shoulders and tried to roll away.

But it was too late. With an iron grip the claws closed around his neck and squeezed. "You stole my bear!" the creature hissed in its strange toneless voice. "And now you—must die."

Steven tried to scream again, but no sound came out. He gasped for breath. He could feel his tongue beginning to swell, and he was suddenly conscious of a tremendous thirst. Frantically his fingers scrabbled at the monster's wrists.

It was no use. Her powerful arms shook him off as if he were a pesky mosquito.

Steven stared up at her, pleading with his eyes, begging for his life. Hoping she could somehow read his message:

Let me go!

Please, let me go. . . .

The monster stared back, her eyes normally dull eyes suddenly a glinting steely gray. She grunted something that Steven couldn't make out.

The pressure on Steven's neck was awful. Already he thought he was seeing stars in front of his eyes. How long could a person go without air? Two minutes? Three?

An unearthly noise rose from the creature's

throat and seemed to float in the darkness above Steven's head. Her weight pressed down on Steven's body. Steven struggled to breathe. *This can't be the end,* he thought in despair. *It—just—can't—*

"My—bear." What remained of the monster's lips curved into a terrible mocking smile.

The bear! Steven knew it was his last chance. Already he was light-headed. In his mind he could feel himself beginning to spiral down, down, down, along a staircase that he knew could only lead to certain death. *The bear!* Summoning all his strength, he lifted up the arm that still held Eva's teddy bear.

With a triumphant cry Eva let go of Steven's neck and reached for the stuffed bear. Air rushed into Steven's lungs, but he couldn't enjoy it. He knew he didn't have much time. Flicking his wrist, he tossed the bear just beyond Eva's reach. Then he bucked like a wild horse.

"Aaaaah!" Caught off balance, Eva tumbled to the ground with an inhuman cry. Steven stood up, panting hard. He knew he ought to run for it, but he felt too weak. *Oh, man.* He sucked in a deep gulp of fresh cool air. He'd never realized what a great feeling it was to be able to breathe.

Eva's clawlike hand shot out and grabbed her bear. Pressing it close to her side, she made cooing noises at it. Then she whirled and faced Steven.

"Hey, man," Steven said nervously, taking a step back. He was dimly aware of blood trickling down his shoulder. "I gave you the bear, you know."

The figure got up unsteadily and lurched forward again.

The bunny slipper. That must be what she wants. Sweat broke out on Steven's forehead. Bending down, he yanked off the slipper and held it out to the creature.

The monster gurgled. Anger flashed in her leaden eyes.

With a scream louder than the screams of the trick-or-treaters he had been frightening, Steven flung the slipper down the alley. Barefoot, he ran off into the night.

But not before hearing the creature's whispered words:

"You and your sisters will be dead by midnight!"

Mrs. Wakefield let the mutilated photograph drop from her hands. With fumbling fingers she seized the letter.

"I thought she was dead," she whispered in the darkness. "I—I could have sworn—"

She caught herself. *I won't think about it!* she

thought fiercely. For twenty-five years she'd kept the memory of that awful night out of her mind and heart. Twenty-five years—and it only bothered her once in a while.

Only around Halloween.

But her hands had taken on a life of their own. And before she knew it, the letter was open, and she was staring faintly at the first line.

"Dear Alice," it read in the childish handwriting she remembered so well.

I won't read it! Mrs. Wakefield thought frantically. She dropped the letter to the floor so she wouldn't read the message inside.

But not before her eyes had fastened on the signature:

Eva Sullivan.

And despite her best efforts Mrs. Wakefield's mind cast back twenty-five years, to a Halloween night just like this one. . . .

"Good-bye, Mr. and Mrs. Sullivan," twelve-year-old Alice Wakefield said at the door to the old mansion. "I hope you have a nice time."

Mrs. Sullivan smiled faintly. Leaning down, she kissed Eva lightly on the cheek, careful not to smear her lipstick. "Thank you, Alice," she said, and she turned to leave.

"Good night, Mom and Dad," Eva said in her slow, solemn way.

"*Good night, sweetheart.*" *Mr. Sullivan squeezed his daughter's shoulder. "We'll see you tomorrow."*

"*Tomorrow,*" *Eva echoed her father.*

"*Oh, and Alice?*" *Mrs. Sullivan beckoned to the baby-sitter. "Make sure Eva's balcony door is locked tonight, all right?" she asked in a loud whisper. "She's been sleepwalking again."*

Alice nodded. Every time she baby-sat for Eva, she made certain that the balcony door was locked. In fact, she usually checked the door three or four times, just in case. But she didn't say so. "I'll be careful, Mrs. Sullivan."

Mrs. Sullivan bit her lip. "I know you will," she said with a sigh. "It's just that the balcony is three floors up and—"

"*Nothing will happen,*" *Alice promised, nodding soberly. "Enjoy the party."*

When Eva's parents were gone, the house seemed even quieter than usual. Eva was a silent, thoughtful child more interested in playing board games or practicing her cursive handwriting than in yelling and running. Alice often felt that Eva didn't belong in a big, spooky mansion like this. Especially not tonight.

Especially not on Halloween.

"*Did you have a good time trick-or-treating?*" *she asked.*

"*I was a fairy princess,*" *Eva said softly. "But I only went to three houses." She touched Alice's sleeve. "Then I got scared, so we came home."*

"Scared?" Alice stroked the girl's cheek. She knew that Eva was an easily frightened child. Often she woke up with nightmares, calling and screaming for help. Or even worse, sobbing softly in bed until Alice came to check on her. "What was frightening?"

"The—the ghosts. And stuff like that."

"Remember what I told you?" Alice asked in a soothing voice. "They aren't real ghosts—just people dressed up in costumes."

Eva nodded. But her face looked troubled.

"Time to get on your nightgown," Alice said gently. She led the way up the stairs to Eva's room, where she helped Eva change into her favorite nightgown: white, with daisies embroidered onto the fabric.

"And those weren't real monsters out there either?" Eva asked, biting her lip.

Alice shook her head. "Of course not." She put her hand around Eva's shoulders and helped her into bed. "It's only for fun. For Halloween."

Eva's face looked fragile and pinched. "Alice?"

"Yes, Eva?"

Eva frowned up at the ceiling. "I—I don't think I like Halloween very much."

"That's OK," Alice assured her, wondering how in the world a person could not like Halloween. "Maybe someday, when you're older, you'll be ready for it. And you'll like it then."

Eva looked at Alice vacantly. "May I have my bear, please?"

Alice nodded and reached into Eva's neat-as-a-pin closet. She found the almost brand-new bear with the tag that read "This bear is the property of Eva Sullivan." Alice handed Eva the bear.

"I saw a vampire too." Eva didn't look at Alice. "And a—I don't know what, a ghoul."

Alice bent closer. "It was only pretend," she murmured. Her heart ached for the little girl. Eva lived in a big mansion with all the toys she could ever want, but Alice suddenly realized that Eva was a prisoner. A prisoner of her own thoughts. A prisoner of her fears. She swallowed hard.

Eva took a deep breath. "Could I please wear my bunny slippers tonight?"

"Oh, Eva." Alice felt genuine dismay. Eva was proud of her new bunny slippers. The trouble was that they muffled the sound of Eva's feet on the floors, so Alice couldn't hear her when she sleepwalked—and wouldn't know if she were walking into any kind of danger.

"Please?" Eva begged.

Alice shook her head regretfully. "I'm sorry, sweetie. But I have to say no."

"Oh." Eva clutched her bear. "I—I think they would help me sleep."

Alice pressed a finger on her lips. If the slippers would help her sleep . . . she wondered if maybe it would be all right for Eva to wear the slippers . . . if maybe there was a way she could wear them safely.

Suddenly she snapped her fingers. "How about you just wear one?" she asked. "I can't let you have both. But if wearing one to bed would help—" Her bare foot should still make enough noise for me to hear, *she thought.*

Eva managed a weak smile. "All right," she said softly. She took the slipper from Alice's hand and slid it onto her foot as Alice turned off the light.

"Do you need anything else?" Alice whispered, locking the balcony door.

The only answer was a muffled yawn.

"Sleep tight," Alice said. She bent down and kissed Eva on the forehead. Eva murmured something and rolled over. Alice waited till she was sure Eva was asleep. Then she crept silently out the door.

She passed the spare room next to Eva's own, the room that shared an entrance to Eva's balcony. Just to be sure, she walked into the dusty room and checked that door too. It was locked as well.

Alice shuddered, imagining if one of the balcony doors were open, imagining Eva sleepwalking over the rail. The Sullivans had talked about building a higher, stronger railing around the balcony. But they hadn't yet. Alice suspected they were hoping that Eva would outgrow sleepwalking first.

She tiptoed down the stairs. Even so, her footsteps echoed through the house. Tonight of all nights! The last thing a frightened child like Eva needed was to wake up Halloween night, thinking there were spooks in the house. No, Eva, *she found herself repeating in her head.* Trick-or-treaters are not real monsters.

Alice turned on the television in the living room and watched with one eye. From time to time she wondered what her friends were up to. She'd missed the big Halloween party earlier that night, but she was planning to meet up later on with Jim Wilkins, Dyan Robbins, and Walter Egbert. Especially Jim—who was becoming more than just a friend.

After a while Alice got up to change the channel. Then she froze. What was that noise?

It sounded like footsteps in the upstairs hallway.

Eva! Dashing for the spiral stairway, Alice hurried up the steps. But the hall was empty. Frowning, Alice leaned against the banister. "Eva?" she called softly.

A giggle floated down from the third floor. Two giggles. Somewhere above her head a door shut.

Alice turned pale. Her heart fluttered in her chest. It's OK, *she told herself, racing up the steps as fast as she could.* The balcony door's locked! *But somehow that thought didn't make Alice feel any better.*

The third-floor hallway was empty too. But to Alice's dismay, a light was burning in the room next to Eva's. Alice's throat felt dry. Afraid of what she might see, she peeked into the spare room.

No one was there.

She stepped forward. The room seemed normal enough—except—

Alice frowned.

The door to the balcony stood wide open.

All at once Alice heard another giggle from behind her. She took a few hurried steps back into the hall. A ghostly figure was there, waving its arms.

"Whooo-oo-oo!" it cried.

Another ghost rose up next to the first. "I have come to haunt you!" it said—and then dissolved in a fit of giggles.

Alice narrowed her eyes. Great. Somehow her friends had managed to sneak into the house—and to scare her practically to death. "What do you think you're doing?" she demanded.

"Pretty good joke, huh?" Walter Egbert asked, laughing hysterically. "We climbed up the stairs when you weren't watching," he explained. "Make a few noises, close a few doors, get Alice upstairs, scare her out of her mind—"

"We went into that room," Jim Wilkins said, gesturing to the spure room behind him. "And out onto the balcony. Did you know that room has a balcony?"

"And then we came back," Dyan Robbins put in, taking off her white sheet. She grinned. "We wanted to see how soon you'd figure it out."

"Well, I wish you hadn't," Alice shot back. "You guys know Eva gets scared of every little thing! And the Sullivans don't allow me to have guests either!"

"Guests?" Dyan asked innocently. "Hey, no problem. We're not your guests. You didn't invite us!"

"Right," Walter chimed in. "If the Sullivans yell—it's not your fault."

Alice sighed. Somehow she didn't think the Sullivans would buy that excuse. "You need to get out of here, now," she said urgently, pushing Walter toward the stairs.

"Temper, temper!" Walter said playfully. He glanced at the door that led to Eva's room. "Is this the bedroom that opens up onto the balcony?"

"Why do you care?" Alice snapped angrily. "Just get—" She broke off, suddenly realizing what he'd said. "What do you mean, bedroom?" she demanded. A small shiver of fear began to creep upward from her toes. "How did you know it was a bedroom?"

Walter shrugged. "'Cause we looked inside. Is that a crime or something?"

"You did what?" Alice stared at Walter in alarm.

"We looked inside," Walter repeated carelessly. "We pushed the door open a little."

"Just to see what was inside," Dyan added. "But it was only a bedroom, nothing interesting. So we didn't go in." She stared at Alice's face. "What's the matter, Alice? You look like you've just seen a ghost!"

"Ha, ha," Walter said loudly, motioning to his ghost outfit.

Jim took a step toward Alice. "Are you all right?" he asked gently.

But Alice wasn't listening. "And then—" she began,

nervously twisting her hands. "And then you closed the door again, right?"

"Um—" Jim's face clouded over.

That was all Alice needed to hear. She turned and sprinted for Eva's bedroom. Switching on the light, she saw in horror that Eva's bed was empty.

She raised her eyes to the glass door. It stood ajar, letting in the night air. And she saw the sight she'd been dreading for months.

Out on the balcony stood Eva Sullivan, her hair whipped back and forth by the wind, her body swaying as she stepped forward carefully, almost deliberately, in her one pink slipper. The teddy bear was pressed tightly against her side. Eva's eyes were closed. She's sleepwalking, Alice thought in horror.

Already Eva was standing at the edge of the balcony. One more step would take her over the low rail—and over the side.

"Eva!" Alice shouted at the top of her lungs, rushing forward as fast as she possibly could.

Hoping against hope that she wouldn't be too late . . .

Fifteen

◇

"Mom! Mom!"

Steven burst through the front door of his house, panting furiously. He dashed into the darkened kitchen. His mother was slumped forward at the kitchen table. "Mom!" he exclaimed. "I saw—you have to—"

"Steven?" Mrs. Wakefield looked at him with eyes that seemed far, far away.

"Mom!" Steven repeated urgently, clutching his mother's shoulders. "The twins—the monster—" He paused for breath.

"Steven?" Gradually Mrs. Wakefield's eyes focused on his. She pulled away from his grip. "What are you talking about?"

Steven tried hard to get his thoughts in order. "The creature—she tried to—and then—the bear—"

Mrs. Wakefield frowned. She stood up slowly. Steven noticed how sad her eyes looked, how unsteady and tired she seemed. "Steven—is this a joke?" she asked.

"I'm not making it up, Mom!" Steven insisted. "I mean, I know the costume looks ridiculous, but—" He paused for air. "The twins—Mom—she said we're meat! History! She told me so! She said we'd—" He took another shuddering breath.

"Oh, Steven." Mrs. Wakefield shut her eyes and lifted a hand to her forehead. "Please speak more softly. I have a pounding headache."

"A headache?" Steven's incredulous voice echoed through the kitchen. "Look, Mom!" he said, bending to show her the scratches on his throat. If she saw them, she'd understand for sure. "I'm sorry about your headache, but this is life and death!"

But Mrs. Wakefield didn't look at him. Instead she shut her eyes and leaned, exhausted, against the kitchen counter. "Steven," she repeated tonelessly. "I think you've let Halloween go to your head."

"Mom!" Steven couldn't think of a way to get through to her. "Where are the girls?" he yelled in a voice much louder than he'd intended.

"Trick-or-treating," Mrs. Wakefield said, pressing her hands to her ears. "Steven, if you'll excuse me—"

But Steven didn't wait. He turned and dashed out the door. Scarcely even noticing that he was barefoot, he sprinted down Calico Drive. He'd never felt so panicked in his entire life.

Somehow he would have to find his sisters by himself. Somewhere on the streets and sidewalks of Sweet Valley. Sometime before midnight. Before—

Before the monster finds them, he thought grimly as he gathered speed.

"OK, gang," Winston announced. "The category is—drumroll, please—girls' names!" He glanced proudly around the room. "We'll start with *A* and go through the alphabet. Each team has five seconds. Jessica and Amy—you're first. Go!"

Jessica sighed. No one else had wanted to play this stupid game, but Winston had insisted. He had appointed himself master of ceremonies, and it was clear that he was enjoying himself thoroughly. She wished she could say the same for herself. "Um—*A* is for Amy, I guess," she said, wondering what she would do if a monster came through the window.

"Alice," Elizabeth put in for the other team.

Alice. Jessica hoped her mom wasn't too miserable tonight. Once again she wondered what could have made her hate Halloween so much.

"*B!*" Winston cried loudly.

"Barbara," Todd offered.

"Brittany," Amy chimed in.

They were on *C* now. Jessica forced herself to think. "Cassandra?" she suggested.

Elizabeth nodded. "Chelsea," she added. "And *D* is for Dorothy."

"Dyan," Amy put in. "Dyan with a *y*," she added, grinning.

That's right, Jessica thought, glancing at her partner. *Dyan's her mother's name.*

"So far it's a tie," Winston said, pretending to speak into a microphone. "And now, ladies and gentlemen, we're on the very difficult letter of *E*. May I remind you that the category is girls' names. Ready? Go!"

"Elizabeth," Elizabeth said automatically.

Jessica wrinkled her nose. She thought hard. *E . . . E . . . E. Edward—that's a boy's name. No good.*

"Elmer?" Amy asked doubtfully.

"Boy," Winston said, checking his watch. "Three—two—"

I have a friend with an E name, Jessica thought, disgusted with herself for not being able to come up with it. *Not Janet or Lila. E is for—*

"Eva!" Amy called out.

Winston drew in his breath sharply. Jessica felt her whole body go suddenly rigid, and Amy clapped her hand to her mouth. "I didn't mean it," Amy said quickly. "Not—not Eva. I meant—" She hesitated.

Jessica racked her brain for her friend's name. E—L—

"Ellen!" Jessica shouted. *Of course, Ellen Riteman.*

Todd smiled tentatively. "*E* is for Ellen," he said, running his tongue along dry lips. "Yeah. I think I like that one a little better."

Jessica sighed deeply. Her body relaxed. Amy had spoken Eva's name—and Eva hadn't showed up. Maybe there was hope after all.

"Ellen. Excellent, excellent name." Winston cleared his throat. "Next letter is—*F!*"

This time Jessica was ready. "Fiona!" she called out.

That's strange.

Jessica suspected her mind was playing tricks on her. She stood outside the bathroom on the second floor of the sprawling mansion, listening hard. She could almost have sworn she'd heard her sister call her name.

Except that her sister was downstairs with the other baby-sitters. In the living room where Jessica had left them, just a few minutes before, to use the bathroom.

Wasn't she?

And this voice was calling from the third floor.

So it must have been my imagination, Jessica

decided. She turned toward the spiral staircase and the relative safety of downstairs. She smiled weakly to herself. *Guess I'm kind of jumpy and—*

"Jessica?"

Jessica snapped to attention. It *was* Elizabeth's voice. Well—almost Elizabeth's voice. Elizabeth's and yet not quite Elizabeth's. *Higher and thinner and—more mushy, somehow.* "Lizzie?" she asked, her own voice quavering.

"This way." It wasn't a question.

"Elizabeth?" Jessica asked again. Making sure the lights in the hallway were burning brightly, she took a few steps toward the voice, wondering what her sister was doing up here. "Is something the matter?"

"Yes," the voice told her. "Come!"

Heart pounding, Jessica walked to the end of the corridor and up the stairs. At the top all she could see was the secret room and next to it a closed door with faint scratches around the knob. Quickly passing Eva's old bedroom, she stood outside the other door. "Where are you, Lizzie?" she asked nervously, expecting someone—or something—to leap out at her at any moment.

"In here." The muffled voice came from directly in front of her.

In there? Jessica stared blankly at the door. She'd seen it before, but she'd never seen the room that lay behind it. She didn't have a clue what might be inside. "Elizabeth!" she called urgently. The idea of entering the room, whatever it was, made her cringe. "What are you *doing?*"

There was no answer.

Biting her lip, Jessica gently put her ear against the door. But she could hardly hear a thing. Only the faint hissing of water running through pipes somewhere in the house. "Elizabeth!" she called softly, rapping on the door. "Let's go back!"

Silence.

Jessica longed to rush back downstairs, to find Todd and Winston and Amy and get their help. But she didn't dare leave her sister. "Elizabeth?" Her voice was trembling. With one hand she tried the doorknob.

To her surprise, the door opened easily. Jessica found herself staring into almost total darkness. Throwing the door open as wide as possible, Jessica blinked in the dim light. There was an old bed and a few broken-looking chairs—it was a storage room, she decided. "Elizabeth!" she called, stepping into the room. "Where are you?"

There was a sudden movement, and the door banged shut behind Jessica. A voice echoed from a pitch-black corner. "Hello, dear sister," it said mockingly.

Jessica screamed.

It wasn't Elizabeth at all.

And that hissing sound she heard hadn't been

water flowing through the pipes either. How could she have been so stupid?

She felt, rather than saw, Eva Sullivan reach out her hand. . . .

Jessica's world went black. Her eyes snapped shut, and she slid to the ground in a dead faint.

"She's been gone, like, ten minutes," Elizabeth said anxiously to her friends. They'd gotten as far as Q in their game, but Elizabeth couldn't begin to think of another name until Jessica returned downstairs.

"It's been only four," Amy corrected her, looking at her watch.

"I thought I heard footsteps earlier," Todd said, his mouth a thin, straight line.

"She—she might be in trouble," Elizabeth muttered, twisting a lock of hair around her finger. She stood up, wondering if she should go search for her sister.

Wondering if she dared.

"Or she might be brushing her hair," Winston said dryly. "We said we'd give her five minutes. Wait thirty more sec—"

Somewhere upstairs a door slammed. There was a loud, terrified scream.

And then there was an appalling silence.

Elizabeth's feet moved almost before she knew it. "The third floor," she shouted. "Hurry!" She dashed for the spiral staircase, her friends at her heels.

"Jessica?" Amy called into the darkness.

"She'd better be all right," Todd muttered.

Elizabeth felt as if her lungs were on fire. Once on the second floor she ran for the little back stairs that led up to the secret room. *The secret room . . .* She hoped that Jessica hadn't gotten in there somehow. She took the steps two at a time.

"But—how did she—" Winston grunted behind her.

Elizabeth didn't say a word. Throwing open the door to the secret room, she stared in silence while the others crowded around. "Jessica!" Amy shouted desperately.

No one answered.

"Next door, maybe?" Todd pointed to the closed door next to what had once been Eva's old bedroom.

"That's strange." Elizabeth gazed at the bulletin board above Eva's old desk. She swallowed hard. The last time she had been in this room, there had been a photograph on the board. A picture of Eva with a girl named Alice. A girl who looked a lot like her mother at age twelve.

And now the picture was gone.

"I heard a whimper from the next room." Amy grabbed Elizabeth's arm. "Do you think it might be—"

Jessica, Elizabeth finished in her mind. She tore her gaze away from the missing photograph. "Let's go!" she hissed, darting back into the hall.

"I still want to know," Winston wheezed, "what Jessica's—doing up here."

Elizabeth didn't bother to answer. There wasn't time. Without thinking twice she pushed open the door of the next room and ran in.

What had started out as a sprint for Steven was becoming more of a marathon. He didn't know how much longer he could keep going. Sweat oozed from every pore. His feet were hacked and bleeding from pounding over the sidewalks. His body ached from thirst, and his breath was coming in heavy, uneven gasps.

But he couldn't stop now. *Where are the twins?* he wondered desperately. And tonight would have to be Halloween—the one evening of the year when everybody was in costume and the streets were jammed. He'd already tackled two blond girls, suspecting that they might be his sisters. One had threatened to sue. Luckily Steven had disappeared into the night before she could get his name and address.

Ahead of him Steven saw a ballerina about Jessica's size and shape in the middle of a large group of kids. "Jessica!" he shouted frantically, but his voice was so weak, he could scarcely hear himself. *It's got to be her,* he thought, his tongue feeling swollen in his mouth.

And even if it isn't, I have to try, don't I? Dashing forward, he hurled himself on the group from behind. "Jessica!" he shouted. With a tackle that would have jarred the biggest quarterback in the NFL, he knocked the ballerina onto the grass.

And then he gulped.

It wasn't Jessica at all.

"What do you think you're doing?" The ballerina rolled over and stared in horror at her knees. "You've ruined my costume!" she shrieked. "It cost six hundred and fifty dollars, and now it's got grass stains—and you've probably torn the tutu too!" She looked warily at Steven. "You owe me big bucks, buddy."

Six hundred and fifty dollars for a costume? Steven got up slowly, wondering who would shell out that kind of cash for Halloween. But when he got a better look at the ballerina, it all made sense: it was Lila Fowler.

Oops. I guess she doesn't really look too much like Jessica, Steven thought. For instance, her hair, pulled back into a tight bun, was brown and not blond. But Steven didn't have time to stand around apologizing. "Where's Jessica?" he demanded, panting for breath.

Lila arched an eyebrow and looked Steven up and down. She clearly didn't know who he was.

"You mean Jessica Just-call-me-baby-sitter Wakefield?" Her voice was heaped high with scorn. "She was with us for, like, ten minutes. Then off she went to baby-sit. I mean, can she please get a life?"

Baby-sitting. Of course! Steven would have smacked himself on the forehead if it wouldn't have taken so much energy. "Thanks, Lila," he said with a groan, dashing toward the Riccoli house.

"Hey, I think I've figured it out. You're Steven!" Lila called after him. "Nice nightgown!"

Sixteen

"Jessica!" Elizabeth knelt over her sister's body, feeling frantically for a pulse. "Jessica, speak to me!"

Jessica moaned but didn't open her eyes. "Who—who are you?" she muttered.

"I think she must have hit her head," Winston commented.

Elizabeth squeezed her sister's hand. "It's Elizabeth," she whispered. "It's going to be OK." With Todd's help she got Jessica into a sitting position on the floor.

Jessica groaned. Gingerly she touched her cheek. "I—I—" She looked around and blinked. "Where am I?"

"Upstairs in the Riccolis'," Elizabeth said. "Next to the secret room."

"It's a storage room, I think," Amy added, staring at the decrepit furniture and the boxes piled here and there. She shivered. "Yuck. It gives me the creeps."

"What happened?" Elizabeth asked. She hooked her arm under Jessica's shoulder, ready to help her sister to her feet.

"I—I—" Jessica shook her head. "I don't know. I thought I heard your voice, and then—" Her face clouded over. "I—I don't remember."

"It's OK," Elizabeth said. She heaved a sigh of relief. At least Jessica wasn't badly hurt. "We'll help you downstairs and—"

She stopped suddenly. A flash of white fabric caught Elizabeth's eye, and she heard a faint hissing sound. *Oh, man!* Letting go of Jessica's shoulder, she dived for the door, her heart in her mouth.

But she was too late.

The door swung shut with a terrible bang. To Elizabeth's ears, it sounded like the closing of a dungeon cell. The room was completely dark, and a chilling laugh erupted from what had been the open doorway.

"Easy bait," the creature hissed. The words were slurred and hard to understand, but Elizabeth had no doubt who was talking.

A footstep sounded on the floor, followed by a sliding sound. Elizabeth stood in terror, trying to figure out where the creature was—and how she could defend herself.

"And now," Eva Sullivan purred in the darkness, "I've got you all just where I want you."

No time to stop and ring the doorbell, Steven decided. The porch light of the Riccoli house was burning brightly. He'd just have to hope that the door would be unlocked.

And that everyone inside was safe.

Steven hit the door with a crash and tumbled into the front hall. "Elizabeth?" he called wildly, pulling himself up and grabbing a pair of boots in case he had to protect himself from Eva. "Jessica?"

There was no answer.

Steven's heart started beating double time. "Jessica!" he shouted, dashing into the living room. "Elizabeth!"

The living room was empty too.

Steven rubbed his throat where Eva had clawed him earlier. It still hurt. "They couldn't have just walked away," he said to himself. Not even his sisters would do something so totally irresponsible.

Would they?

Elizabeth backed up slowly, her fingers probing in the darkness for Eva Sullivan. Her head spun. To be shut up in a room with a girl of amazing strength—and not even to know where that girl *was* . . .

The room was totally, horribly dark and just as silent. Elizabeth strained to hear the hissing noise, the faint shuffling sound, but there was nothing.

Don't scream, she told herself firmly, hoping she had the willpower to heed her own command. *If you make a noise now, she'll know where you are. And she'll be on you in a second.* In her mind's eye she could see Eva reaching forward with her long fingernails, her long *pointed* fingernails, and scratching a deep gouge in Elizabeth's leg—

And Elizabeth would never even see her enemy coming.

As silently as she could Elizabeth drew in her breath and took another step back. Her fingers brushed something soft. Soft and fuzzy. Fabric of some kind. Like—maybe—a nightgown.

Elizabeth couldn't stop herself.

"Help!" she shouted in terror.

Downstairs, Steven started. The cry for help was some distance away, that was for sure. *Probably upstairs,* he thought. And it was so faint, he wasn't even positive it was one of his sisters. But still—

If someone needs help, I've got to go, he thought.

He pounded up the spiral steps, three at a time.

After all, he thought grimly, *I'm the only one around!*

"I'm too *young* to die!" Winston cried.

"Save me, save me!" Jessica wailed.

Elizabeth felt silly for having screamed so loudly. The fabric was only a worn blanket draped on the bed, she realized—not Eva's nightgown at all.

But her cry had unleashed something in the other baby-sitters. Jessica's wails echoed and re-echoed in the closed room. Elizabeth's grip tightened on a chair. Maybe she could use it to push her way toward the door. Her mouth felt dry. She tugged experimentally on the chair, just to see if it would move.

It could work. It might work. Only—which way was the door? Elizabeth's eyes darted this way and that, but it was too dark to see.

And then, almost in her ear, she heard the hissing. . . .

Elizabeth had just opened her mouth to scream when footsteps sounded in the corridor. In a flash the door swung open wide. Light from the hallway flooded the room. Elizabeth stood transfixed, blinking in the harsh brightness.

Not two feet from her elbow, there stood Eva
Sullivan.

And in the doorway, panting hard, stood yet
another Eva Sullivan.

Only taller. And without a bunny slipper.

This is the end, she thought. Her shoulders
sagged. Her blood turned to ice.

And a scream—louder than any she had ever
heard before—rose from her lips.

With a satisfying crunch Steven knocked the
small figure in the nightgown to the floor. Any
ref would have given him a penalty for unnecessary roughness. But this wasn't football. This was
real life.

Besides, he figured that there was no such
thing as "unnecessary" roughness where Eva
Sullivan was concerned.

"Let's get out of here!" he yelled to his sisters
and their friends. "Come on! Move!"

Nobody moved. They just clutched each other
and stared at Steven as if he had horns.

"I'm too *nice* to die!" Winston wailed. "I'm too
strong to die! I'm too—"

"There can't be two of her," Amy whispered.

Two of her! Of course! Steven's hand flew to
his face. "I'm Steven," he cried. "In costume, you
idiots! *She's* the one who's trying to kill you!"
He pointed to Eva, who was already stirring.

"Get it into gear—now!" he bellowed.

Screaming, the kids surged past him and through the door. With a snarl Eva leaped to her feet. Steven didn't hesitate. Following his sisters, he yanked the door shut and held it tight. "Out of the house!" he ordered. "Run!"

"The kids!" Elizabeth turned a teary face toward him.

"What kids?" Steven yelled. Eva was tugging at the door. "Get out of here, now!"

"The Riccoli kids!" Jessica's fists clenched and unclenched. "We've got to save them too!"

Steven gritted his teeth and pulled his end of the door as hard as he could. "OK," he agreed. "Just hurry!"

Like scared rabbits, the baby-sitters darted downstairs.

"Essica?" Nate opened his eyes and yawned.

"I'm here, sweetie," Jessica murmured. She stood by the little boy's crib, cradling him in her arms as she waited for the other baby-sitters.

Nate closed his eyes again almost instantly. In less than ten seconds he was breathing evenly, his head against Jessica's shoulder.

Jessica watched him sleep with envy. She wished someone would take care of her like this. Above her head she could hear the banging of the door to the storage room—and then a sudden *oof* from Steven. Her heart sank.

"She's loose!" Steven appeared on the stairs, barely recognizable under his heavy, gruesome makeup. He hurried to Jessica's side and pushed her farther into the darkness. "Hide!"

A second passed. Then Eva lurched down the stairs. Jessica shrank back, hoping that Nate wouldn't cry and give them away. But Eva didn't even look around. Instead she swayed to the top of the spiral staircase and wobbled down toward the first floor. In a second she was out of sight.

Jessica shot Steven a glance, afraid to hope. The other baby-sitters and the rest of the Riccoli kids, yawning and stretching, were in the hallway now.

"I'll go first," Steven said under his breath. "If I see her, I'll whistle. Jessica, count to ten and follow behind."

Jessica nodded. Nate was still asleep in her arms. She was grateful for that.

Steven took a step forward, then another and another. But about halfway down the corridor he hesitated and sniffed the air. Jessica's heart skipped a beat.

"What is it?" Todd hissed.

Steven spun around. Beneath his makeup Jessica could tell his face was white as a sheet.

She sniffed the air too—and smelled something burning.

"Can't you tell?" Steven asked weakly. "She's set the house on fire. We can't get out."

Steven turned back toward the spiral steps. "And—" He swallowed hard.

"And she's coming upstairs right now."

Elizabeth choked back a sob. The cloud of acrid smoke was already beginning to waft into the hallway. "The study window," she said, her voice quavering.

"The what?" Steven snapped.

"The study window," Elizabeth repeated, more sure of herself now. "The roof, um, slopes pretty gently there, and there's, like, an awning that goes almost down to the ground." She sketched pictures in the air. Somehow she was having trouble speaking. "We can get the kids out there. I think."

Eva Sullivan's misshapen head appeared around the curve of the steps. Her hissing seemed louder than ever.

There was no time to lose. Elizabeth led the way, dragging Juliana behind her as she made a mad dash for the study.

"It's a long way down," Todd said, staring out the study window. He set his jaw. "And it's a very small window."

"We don't have a choice." Elizabeth's voice was firm. Already Eva was pounding on the locked door. "She'll break in any minute. And there's the fire too." Her heart was beating so furiously, she practically expected it to burst from her chest.

Steven studied the roof with a practiced eye. "All right," he said. "Riccolis first." Grabbing Olivia's hand, he hoisted her up and swung her into the inky blackness of the night.

Elizabeth held her breath. But Olivia didn't disappoint her. Like a spider, she climbed down the roof and onto the awning. Then she dropped safely to the ground. "OK, I can catch the next one!" she called, opening her arms wide.

Elizabeth felt like cheering. She pushed Andrew forward. "Did you see how Olivia did it, sweetie?" she asked, more to cover the noise of Eva's incessant pounding than to explain. "You grab on there, see, and—"

"I can *do* it," Andrew said as Steven passed him quickly through the window. Elizabeth watched him steady himself on the shingles. But instead of clambering down to join his sister, Andrew reached back toward the sill. "Hey, guys," he said quickly. "Um—I'll take Nate down with me, OK?"

"Are you sure?" Jessica's voice sounded shaky, but she handed the little boy through the window to his older brother.

Elizabeth watched, her heart in her mouth. Andrew moved slowly and carefully. Holding Nate to his chest, he made his way to the awning. Then he gave the toddler to Olivia and swung down himself.

Yes! Elizabeth wanted to shout. Hope rose in her chest. But the banging on the door was louder and more violent. And the door was straining on its hinges.

"Your turn." Steven grabbed Juliana and half flung her onto the roof.

"Faster!" Todd pleaded, taking a quick look behind him. Biting her lip, Elizabeth helped Gretchen out the window just behind her sister. Plumes of smoke curled into the room. But Gretchen would make it, she was sure.

They'd saved the Riccolis.

Now to save themselves.

Jessica was peering out the window, watching Gretchen tumble to the ground, when she heard an awful cracking sound. Whirling around, she saw the frame of the door begin to splinter. As if in slow motion, chunks of wood crashed to the floor. Jessica felt panic rise in her throat.

"Me first!" Winston pushed in front of Jessica and started to dive through the window. Jessica caught her breath. It would be a tight squeeze.

There was a victorious cry from the doorway.

Jessica spun around—to see Eva Sullivan's face appear in the exact spot where the heavy wooden door had just been.

"Help me!" Winston cried desperately. His body was wedged impossibly against the sill, his legs dangling. "Is that her? I can't get through!"

Jessica couldn't bear to look at the mocking smile on Eva's face. Suppressing a scream, she watched as Eva stepped slowly forward.

There was only one thing to do. She grabbed Winston by the legs and yanked him as hard as she could. In a second he was out of the window, back inside. Jessica steadied herself against the sill. She didn't dare look behind her.

"Run!" she shouted, leaning as far out as she dared. It was no wonder Winston had gotten stuck; the window was much smaller than it looked. "Run! Get help!"

The children stared up at her from the lawn, openmouthed.

Jessica knew she had little time left. "Run!" she cried again. "Hurry! As fast as you can!"

Olivia nodded. Or at least Jessica hoped she did. And in a moment the kids were scurrying across the lawn in their pajamas, heading—

Jessica didn't know where. Just now there were more important things on her mind. She turned and screamed. The monster was lunging at her neck.

"No!" she cried.

Eva's claws grasped Jessica's throat.

With a sickening thud Jessica fell to the floor. Her thoughts spun wildly as she felt the sharp fingernails tighten, ever so slowly, around her windpipe. Painfully she breathed in a tiny mouthful of air—

Wondering if it would be her last breath on earth.

Seventeen

Mrs. Wakefield squeezed her eyes shut. But the image of Eva poised at the edge of the balcony wouldn't go away. Even after Steven had stormed in, babbling about goodness-only-knew what, Mrs. Wakefield couldn't get rid of that dreadful picture.

Taking a deep breath, she wrapped her head in her arms and slumped forward against the kitchen table.

She had to relive the rest of the nightmare.

She had no other choice. . . .

"Eva!" Alice cried, sprinting toward the sleepwalking girl.

Eva stepped over the low rail, her bunny-slippered foot groping in the darkness for solid ground.

"Eva!" Alice's heart pounded.

Could she make it in time?

Eva opened her eyes for a fraction of a second. Turning her head, she met Alice's gaze with a faint smile. She clutched her teddy bear tightly to her chest, even as her body leaned forward into the empty air, bending toward the ground three stories below.

The wind whipped Eva's nightgown around her legs. Her arm reached out as if to steady herself. But there was nothing to steady herself against.

"Grab her!" Jim shouted.

"Eva!" Alice's cry stuck in her throat. Forcing her way onto the balcony, she reached for the sleepwalking girl.

But like an autumn leaf, Eva began to fall—

Alice's scream pierced the night. Her fingers grabbed at nothing. She stretched her body forward and stared in horror at the spot where the little girl had been standing just a split second before.

From the ground there came an appalling sound, a sound that would ring in Alice's dreams for years to come. The sound of a human body crashing into the earth.

No, not just "a human body." Eva.

Stunned, Alice peered over the railing, only to see the little girl's broken, twisted body, lying oh so silently on the dirt three stories below.

From behind her Alice heard screams. She leaned out into the wind, hoping for a sign of movement, but there was none. Helpless tears stung Alice's eyes. It can't be, it can't be. Oh, please—

Alice's face grew hot, and her stomach churned. But worse yet was the terrible, sudden feeling of emptiness as she stared at Eva. At what had once been a living, breathing little girl.

And since that moment, Mrs. Wakefield realized, nothing had ever been quite the same again. . . .

She sat motionless, her head still in her hands. The world seemed very dark now, very dark and very lonely. When Eva had fallen, it had been like a candle going out.

Yet the shadow of the candle's flame, she thought, was still very much alive.

And what had happened next? Mrs. Wakefield forced herself to think. Someone had called an ambulance. No, the police. And Mr. and Mrs. Sullivan had come home, and there had been tears and shouts and anguished cries, and—

And there had been a funeral. Yes. Mrs. Wakefield distinctly remembered a funeral. Of course there had been a funeral. Eva was dead. That was obvious. She hadn't moved a muscle while lying on the ground. Even after all those years Mrs. Wakefield remembered that motionless body. She couldn't forget it if she tried. The memory was too clear. Almost as if it were yesterday.

But then—

Her toe brushed a piece of paper on the floor. Mrs. Wakefield exhaled. She knew that she had to read the letter, the letter impossibly signed "Eva Sullivan."

Taking a deep breath, she fished it off the floor and began to read. . . .

Dear Alice,

I bet you thot I was dead, well Im not. I fell all right but I dident die. My mom and dad tok me to a hostable but I excaped. They told peple I was dead and they berried my doll but they did not berry me.

I went to lots of plases but I alwas came back to my house. I staid in a shack and in a old room next to the one that was my bedroom. No body knew I was there not even mom and dad.

Then dad dide and mom dide and the house got soled.

It is your falt you know. Alice it is all your falt and your frends falt. You did not have the rite to fritten me and make me loose my balans on the balconie.

Now other peple have moved into my house. And girls who look like you are here too some times. I scair them Alice. I youse make up so I look like a monstr.

But I am not going to onley scair them now.

Alice I am going to kill them.

I am going to kill them all. Becaus of what you did to me.

Eva Sullivan

The letter was full of rips and cross outs, but Mrs. Wakefield scarcely noticed them. Trembling, she folded the note and slid it carefully into the envelope.

So Eva had not died after all. The truth of it struck her like a bolt of lightning. And at the funeral they had not buried her body. *If she escaped from a hospital,* Mrs. Wakefield told herself, *they all must have figured that she wouldn't get far. They would have assumed she'd died.* She shook her head, marveling at how the girl could have survived the fall to begin with.

But how had Eva ended the letter? "'I am going to kill them all,'" Mrs. Wakefield repeated, running her tongue nervously around her lips.

Something tugged at her memory. Something Steven had said not so very long ago. She'd thought he was just babbling, but maybe not. What was it? *"She said we're meat."* She.

And tonight was Halloween. The anniversary of—

Mrs. Wakefield had pushed back the memories for twenty-five years. But now she knew that if she wanted to save the lives of innocent people, she would have to act—and act *now*.

Her heart beating furiously, she dashed for the phone.

*   *   *

"Hello, Jim," Mrs. Wakefield said softly.

The voice at the other end of the line sounded wary. "Who is this, please?"

Mrs. Wakefield drew in a deep breath. Calling 911 had been the easy part. This call was different: it was like tearing open an old wound that had never really healed. "It's Alice," she said flatly, not allowing a hint of emotion to escape. "And tonight is—Halloween."

There was a sigh. "Yes," Jim Wilkins said as if he'd been expecting this call for many years.

"Listen, Jim." Alice gripped the receiver tightly. "Get to the Sullivan mansion as fast as you can. Our children are in danger." *Our children. All of our children,* she thought. *Winston Egbert—Walter's son. And Dyan's daughter, Amy. And your son Todd and my own daughters.* Her heart thundered in her chest. "It's—Eva."

There was silence on the other end of the line. "This is a joke, right?" Todd's father asked.

"I wish it were, Jim," Mrs. Wakefield said. "Call Walter and Dyan and get over there now." She hung up the phone before Mr. Wilkins could say another word.

And it was at that very moment that the doorbell rang.

"Mrs. Wakefield! Mrs. Wakefield!"

Mrs. Wakefield froze. These were not ordinary

trick-or-treaters. The doorbell rang again and again, as if someone was leaning on it. "Hurry!" a high voice yelled.

Within seconds Mrs. Wakefield had flipped on the lights and pulled open the door. Five children in pajamas and nightgowns stood in the doorway. "It's a monster!" shouted the smallest girl, tears streaming down her face. "She's got them!"

"What? Who?" Mrs. Wakefield looked anxiously from face to face.

The older boy caught his breath. "We're the— Riccolis. Jessica and Elizabeth are—baby-sitting for us. It's an emergency!"

"What?" Mrs. Wakefield grabbed the boy by the shoulders, panic seizing her heart.

"It's the monster from our nightmares," the tallest girl said breathlessly. "The one with the nightgown and the teddy bear. The evil one. She's got Jessica and Elizabeth! She's set fire to the house! She's—"

Mrs. Wakefield didn't wait. She was in the car and backing out the driveway before the girl could finish her sentence.

Eighteen

◇

Elizabeth stared in horror. The monster had her sister by the throat and was squeezing tight. In a second, she knew, it would be too late. *Help Jessica!* her brain commanded again and again. Yet her body wouldn't move.

Jessica's eyes bulged horribly. Her fingers made frantic groping motions, but Eva just shook them off.

"Todd!" All at once Elizabeth's eye lit on Todd in his Orioles uniform. "Your bat! Hit her!"

"My—bat?" Todd's jaw dropped open, and he hefted the baseball bat at his side. Slowly he raised it into a batting stance, holding it tightly with both hands.

"Hurry!" Elizabeth urged. She didn't know how much longer Jessica could last.

Todd didn't hesitate. With a sickening crunch the bat sailed through the air and slammed into Eva's shoulder. There was an anguished wail. In a flash Eva had keeled over onto her side, holding her injured shoulder with her good hand. Her face contorted into an expression of horrible pain.

Elizabeth stepped forward. "Jess!" she exclaimed, offering her sister a hand.

Jessica gurgled and clutched her throat. Weakly she reached for Elizabeth's arm.

"Grab her," Elizabeth hissed to Amy. She kept a wary eye on Eva, moaning in the corner. *Eva's tough,* she thought. *We don't have much time to get away—*

"I—I can't believe I did that." Todd sagged weakly against the wall, staring at his bat.

"What choice did you have?" Steven punched Todd's shoulder. "Nice hit, kid. Double in any ballpark."

"Let's get rolling!" Winston cried. He motioned toward the door. "Now's our chance, and the fire's not going down any!"

Jessica was on her feet. Amy and Elizabeth half pushed, half dragged her to what remained of the door. "Follow me!" Steven shouted, ducking through the splintered wood.

Elizabeth took a quick look behind her. Eva was standing now. One arm hung weakly at her side, but her eyes flashed with renewed anger. "Revenge," she croaked, lurching forward. Her lips parted in an awful grimace. "Re-venge."

"Hurry!" Elizabeth pushed Jessica through the door, wondering what the twins had ever done to Eva to make her seek revenge upon them.

"Oh, man!" Steven's voice rang out. "The stairway down is on fire." He stood motionless in the hallway. "The whole blasted staircase!"

Amy stared. "Now what?" she asked in despair.

Elizabeth breathed deeply, taking in a big mouthful of acrid smoke. Blue and orange flames danced in front of her. Steven was right. The spiral staircase was no way out.

Jessica gurgled again. "Up," she croaked, and she raised a forefinger to point toward the third floor. She coughed violently. "Those— stairs— should be—OK."

"The secret room," Elizabeth said softly. Did they dare? She was afraid that would take them right into Eva's territory.

A tendril of flame curled into the hallway and licked at the base of the banister. There was a faint sizzling sound, and smoke billowed up from the first floor. Elizabeth bit her lip. *What else can we do?* "Follow me!" she shouted, and she turned to sprint for the third floor, helping Jessica along with her.

She looked back only once, to see Eva pounding up the steps after them.

And behind Eva the flames, bright and hot and glowing.

No windows.

Jessica felt like crying. And she might have cried too, if it didn't hurt her throat and her lungs just to breathe. It had been her idea to go to the secret room to escape the fire, her idea to go upstairs—and somehow she had completely forgotten that the secret room had no windows.

She blinked back tears. She glanced around the secret room, her gaze returning again and again to a certain point on the wall opposite the door. *Weird.* She had been positive there was a window in that spot. Not an ordinary window either. A big one, with a sliding glass door out to a balcony or something—

But that must have been only a dream, she realized.

"She's here!" Winston couldn't keep the terror out of his voice.

Jessica whirled around. Eva Sullivan stood in the doorway, one hand outstretched toward the kids. Jessica gulped, seeing the fingers that had nearly shaken the life out of her.

"Revenge," Eva hissed in that horrible low whisper. "Finally my dream has come true." She lifted a bare foot and stepped toward Jessica. Her eyes glittered in the near-darkness. "My dream. Your nightmare."

Jessica smothered a scream. Instinctively she moved back toward the wall. Toward the spot where she had once dreamed there had been an exit.

In the distance the flames crackled.

"Say—your—prayers." Eva spoke calmly and deliberately. She advanced another step.

Jessica backed away again. With one hand she groped for the wall. With the other she fumbled for her sister's. There was a terrible lump in her throat. *Mom,* she thought frantically. *Don't you know that I need you—and fast?*

"We're doomed," Todd said flatly.

Winston grabbed his shoulders. "The bat! Hit her with—"

"It wouldn't do any good now," Todd said. "It's not just her. It's . . . it's the fire."

The smoke was becoming thicker and thicker. Jessica held her breath. Outside the secret room, in the hallway, there was a flash of orange, and downstairs Jessica thought she could hear the distant crash of a beam in another part of the house.

Eva swung around. "Forget the fire," she snarled. "You will be dead before it reaches you!" And with a sudden unearthly scream she charged directly at the twins.

The next moment Jessica felt herself being shoved violently backward, powerless against Eva's amazing strength. The same thing was happening to Elizabeth, she saw dimly out of the corner of her eye. Jessica clawed the air. "Help!" she cried.

But it was no use. There was a splintering crash as Jessica hit the wall, Elizabeth at her side. Jessica tensed her body, waiting to rebound to the floor. But to her surprise, the wall behind her began to give. The plaster crumbled around her. And then all at once there was a gust of fresh air on her head. *I've broken through,* she thought numbly.

"Jessica!" someone shouted above her.

Jessica clutched her sister's hand tighter than ever. She felt completely weightless. To her horror, she realized that they were falling, hurtling through the air with increasing speed. Jessica tumbled down and down and down toward the cold hard earth below.

I hope it won't hurt very much, she thought, squeezing Elizabeth's hand for reassurance.

And then there was nothing to do but to wait for the blow that would knock the life from her— forever.

Nineteen

Elizabeth lay still as still could be. *How . . .
strange.* When she had landed on the ground
after what seemed like hours in the air, the earth
had been somehow—soft.

She lay on her back, staring up into the night
sky, wondering if she was dead or alive. Beside
her Jessica stirred slightly. Elizabeth shivered.
The air was cold. *Does it get chilly in heaven?* she
wondered.

She took a deep breath.

"Elizabeth?" The voice sounded anxious.
"Elizabeth, honey, are you all right?"

Mom's voice, Elizabeth suddenly realized. And
there was her mother's face, worried, anxious,
near tears, hovering over her own, and her
mother's arms tucked gently around her head

and shoulders. "Oh, Elizabeth," Mrs. Wakefield gasped.

"Mom?" Elizabeth sat bolt upright, wondering what on earth her mother was doing here. "But how—"

Other arms surrounded her. Elizabeth felt herself being moved gently onto harder ground nearby. With a start she looked down. Grass. "It's OK," someone in a firefighter's uniform told her. "You'll be fine."

Elizabeth stared openmouthed at the mattress she and her sister had landed on. Her stomach clenched as she thought of what could have happened if the mattress hadn't been there. Behind her there were strange flashing lights. Emergency vehicles, she decided.

Besides her mother and the firefighters there were other adults too. A police officer, and an ambulance driver, and Todd's dad, and Amy's mother, and she thought she could make out Winston's father, looking grim.

My friends. Elizabeth gulped. Suddenly she remembered her friends and her brother, trapped up there in the burning house with Eva Sullivan. She raised a shaky finger, amazed and horrified by what she saw.

The house was burning brightly, blazing like a candle in the wind. Smoke streamed from almost every window, and as Elizabeth listened she could hear the crackle of flames and the snapping of wood. Her gaze traveled up to the third floor. There was a gaping hole in the side of the house, and in the hole, silhouetted against the advancing flames, stood Todd Wilkins.

Sirens wailed in the distance. Elizabeth squeezed her eyes shut tight and clung to her sister's hand. The firefighters might be here already, but this fire seemed too out of control to tame.

"Jump!" Mr. Wilkins was shouting frantically. "Jump, Todd!"

Elizabeth opened her eyes in time to see Todd bend his knees and launch himself off the roof. With a drawn-out cry he tumbled down—and onto the mattress, where he landed with a thud. In a second two firefighters had grabbed him and pulled him to safety.

Elizabeth stared up at the rubble of what had once been the wall of the secret room. In turn Amy and Winston also jumped through the hole in the wall and landed safely on the mattress.

"Where's Steven?" Elizabeth's heart was thumping quicker than ever. She stared up at the fiery building, biting her lip. Already the flames were shooting up from the roof. *It's got to be a thousand degrees in there,* she thought, trying not to panic. *And he was only there to rescue me and my friends. . . .*

If he dies, she thought, *it will be all my fault.*

A figure appeared on the wall, scrambling to maintain its balance against the onrushing flames. A nightgown billowed around its knees, and even from a distance Elizabeth could tell that its face was scarred and bruised. "Eva," she half whispered. There were knots in her stomach.

"Eva," Jessica echoed her blankly.

"No!" Todd grabbed her shoulder. "It's not Eva! It's too tall! It's Steven!"

Steven! Elizabeth's heart sang. She'd forgotten all about his costume. But now that Todd mentioned it, she could make out her brother's features as clear as day. "Jump!" she shouted.

"Jump!" the other kids chorused.

Steven flung himself off the edge of the burning house. His legs bicycled frantically in the air as he tried to keep his balance. Down he plunged—down, farther and farther—

But Elizabeth didn't see her brother land. Something above his head caught her attention:

Another figure up in the house. Shorter than Steven.

But dressed the same way.

While all the adults clustered around Steven, Elizabeth stared at the hole in the secret room, where Eva Sullivan stood, her lips frozen into a silent scream, her arms stretched out as if pleading to be saved.

There was a sudden crash. Elizabeth watched, shading her eyes. As if in slow motion, the roof fell in. Charred shingles came sliding to the ground with a heavy thunk.

Flames shot up triumphantly across the entire house.

Elizabeth longed to tear her eyes away, but she couldn't. Outlined against the fire, Eva clutched what remained of the wall. The girl's fingers scrambled for a handhold. Sparks flew all around her body, burning the white nightgown as they fell.

Elizabeth stared. She was sure she saw fear in those dull eyes. Above the roar of the chimney collapsing, Elizabeth thought she could make out a terrified wail coming from the third floor.

Flames licked at the rubble where the wall had once stood. With a heartrending cry, Eva staggered backward and disappeared into the inferno.

Elizabeth shut her eyes tight. She buried her head in her hands and cried. *I can't imagine why I'm crying*, she thought as tears stained her cheeks. *The nightmare is over and yet—*

And yet in a sad, terrible, awful way, she felt unbearably sorry that Eva Sullivan wasn't going to make it.

When she opened her eyes a few seconds later, the entire mansion was engulfed in flames.

Twenty

◇

"So Eva was really alive, after all," Jessica said slowly. It was a week later, and she and Elizabeth were in the car, driving with their mother to Sweet Valley Meadows Cemetery.

Mrs. Wakefield nodded soberly, but she kept her eyes firmly locked on the road. "Yes, she was."

"If you can call it living," Elizabeth put in. She shuddered, thinking about what Eva must have gone through during the last twenty-five years. "It's just like Miss Havisham, isn't it? Eva never got over what happened that Halloween night."

Jessica twisted a lock of hair. "But I still don't really understand how come she didn't die, Mom. I mean—if she was all banged up like that . . ."

Mrs. Wakefield signaled a left turn into the cemetery gates. "I doubt we'll ever know the whole story, but I did manage to find out a little about what happened," she said. "Eva was badly injured, all right, but she wasn't dead. They took her to a hospital, one specializing in rehabilitation."

"Reha what?" Jessica asked, frowning.

"Where they try to help injured people use their bodies again," Elizabeth explained. "It would have been an awful job with Eva," she guessed, shaking her head sadly as she remembered how badly damaged Eva's tiny body had been.

"Actually Eva's injuries weren't as bad as you think," Mrs. Wakefield explained.

"Really?" Jessica frowned. "Her face and her hands looked pretty awful to me," she said.

Mrs. Wakefield nodded. "But some of that was only makeup. She tried to make herself look as disfigured as she could."

"Oh." Elizabeth stared thoughtfully out the window. That would explain why Steven was able to get his own face to look exactly like Eva's. She gazed out across the grave markers. Out there somewhere, she knew, Eva Sullivan was now really and truly buried. "But didn't they tell you that she was still alive, Mom?"

"It would have been nice," Mrs. Wakefield agreed. "And to be honest, girls, maybe they did.

I wasn't in great shape for a while back then."
She was silent a moment, remembering. "They
were going to try to fix Eva's broken bones so
they would heal properly, and there was a problem with her windpipe—"

"The hissing sound," Elizabeth said.

Mrs. Wakefield nodded. "But Eva wasn't at
the rehabilitation place for long."

"She wasn't?" Jessica leaned forward.

Mrs. Wakefield shook her head. "There was a
river at the back of the hospital, a river with dangerous currents. Several children had drowned
there."

"They let Eva go swimming?" Elizabeth asked
incredulously.

"No," Mrs. Wakefield replied. "But a few days
after she arrived, Eva somehow wandered off.
The nurse I talked to still remembers it. She said
Eva's injuries were awful, really horrendous, and
it was amazing that she could have walked three
steps on her own, let alone gotten all the way
outside."

"Well, Eva had a lot of determination," Jessica
said slowly.

"That's for sure." Elizabeth shivered.

"Anyway," Mrs. Wakefield went on, "Eva sim-
ply—disappeared. Some of her possessions were
found on the river's edge. A doll, a blanket, a few
other things."

"I get it," Jessica said. "When she didn't turn up, they just assumed she must have fallen in and drowned."

"That's right," Mrs. Wakefield agreed. "And because they couldn't find the body, they decided to bury the doll instead of her."

"But—" Elizabeth was still confused. "Where was she all this time, then? How did she eat? What was she doing?" She was having a hard time keeping her questions in single file.

Mrs. Wakefield pulled to a stop near the Sullivan family plot and put her hand on the door latch. For the first time she looked directly at the twins. "Nobody really knows," she said. "It seems as if she spent some time in the house—"

"In that room next to the secret room, I bet," Jessica said, giving Elizabeth a poke in the side.

"And in that little shack on the Sullivan property," Mrs. Wakefield added. "But she might have gone other places as well."

"In her bunny slipper and nightgown?" Jessica frowned.

"Well, she had other clothes too," Mrs. Wakefield explained. "But those had special meaning for her. You can see why." She grimaced. "And as for eating, it's just possible that the gardener was feeding her."

"Mr. Brangwen." Elizabeth remembered the

old gardener who had dropped dead after giving the girls a warning. *Never shut your eyes in this house,* he had advised them. Elizabeth wrinkled her nose. "He was absolutely right," she murmured.

"Was he feeding her because he was nice?" Jessica demanded. "Or was she threatening him?"

Mrs. Wakefield shrugged. "I don't know," she admitted. "Maybe both."

"And Mrs. Sullivan?" Elizabeth remembered that Eva's mother had died only the previous summer. "Did she know too?"

Mrs. Wakefield hesitated. "I doubt it," she said at last. "Mrs. Sullivan closed up most of the house after her husband died, you know, and she lived in just a few rooms. She never got over the accident either. Neither of the Sullivans did. I'd guess that Eva stayed well out of their way."

Jessica wrung her hands. "So we really *were* seeing Eva," she said quietly.

"And even when we didn't see her, her presence was all around us—kind of like a living ghost," Elizabeth murmured. "It was like Eva was so incredibly angry, she just had kind of a power over everything that went on in the house."

"Like, we'd see her, maybe without even noticing it, and then we'd all dream about her?" Jessica asked.

"Something like that." Elizabeth hesitated. "I was just thinking about that night when we all dreamed we were on the roof. Remember, when I scratched my wrist? Nate woke me up, and he said something about a big, ugly girl. Maybe Eva scratched me in real life, and Nate saw her."

Jessica shook her head. "Eva wasn't exactly big," she pointed out.

"But to a two-year-old like Nate, she would have been," Elizabeth argued.

Jessica drew in a breath. "Maybe you're right. But how would we all have the exact same dream, then?"

"I don't think we'll ever know the answers," Mrs. Wakefield said. "Some things will just remain mysteries forever, and I suspect this may be one of them."

"I guess you're right," Elizabeth murmured.

Jessica made a face. "Eva had never gotten to live a normal life, so she wanted revenge. And if she couldn't get revenge on you and your friends—"

"Then she'd get revenge on us," Elizabeth finished for her. "On us and on your friends' kids."

"And when the house was finally sold and the Riccolis moved in," Mrs. Wakefield said, "that was enough to drive her over the edge." She shook her head. "It's very sad, isn't it?"

Jessica rolled her eyes. "Scary, you mean."

Elizabeth bit her lip. She could understand what both Jessica and her mother were feeling. Eva's story was an awful tragedy. Her life had been horribly wasted. Ruined. And yet Eva had also been responsible for some of the most horrifying nights Elizabeth had ever experienced. "Sad *and* scary," she said.

Opening the door, she got out of the car and stood on the soft green grass of the cemetery.

"Well, that explains a lot," Jessica said. The warm sunshine caressed her cheek. "But there's one thing I don't understand." She turned to her mother. "How did you know what would happen—last week, I mean?"

Mrs. Wakefield sighed. "You know, girls," she said slowly as they walked past the low iron rail that surrounded the Sullivan plot, "I tried so hard to forget about Eva. And I couldn't. Every time I let the memories come back, they would—be just as vivid as ever."

Jessica nodded. "But—"

"Then on Halloween night I had two warnings," Mrs. Wakefield explained. "One was a letter from Eva herself."

"From Eva?" Elizabeth gulped.

"Do you still have the letter?" Jessica asked. Then she shook her head. "Forget it. I don't think I want to see it."

"What was the other warning?" Elizabeth wanted to know.

"It was from Steven," Mrs. Wakefield explained. "He'd tangled with her in an alley—and I hate to admit, I completely ignored him when he tried to tell me what was going on." She put her hand to her temple. "But when I thought about Eva last week, I could see the scene where she fell as clearly as if it were yesterday."

Jessica frowned. "And?" she prompted.

Her mother spread out her hands. "It made sense that that scene would be somehow re-created. So I called Jim and Dyan and Walter. None of us had been in that mansion for twenty-five years. But we all remembered exactly where the balcony was."

"Even though it wasn't there anymore," Jessica said softly. In her mind's eye she remembered how the secret room had been blocked off and the glass door plastered over. *Eva's parents must have done that*, she decided. *They couldn't stand to be reminded of the tragedy, so they walled off their memories*. The idea made Jessica feel a little queasy.

"Even though it wasn't there anymore," Mrs. Wakefield repeated. Her eyes had a faraway look. "So Walter and I kept our eyes trained up on the third floor, and Jim and Dyan found an old mattress in the garage—"

"That was Andrew Riccoli's," Elizabeth broke in. "It was damaged in the first fire."

Mrs. Wakefield nodded. "And we dragged it under the place where the balcony had been." She bit her lip. "And we could hear sirens in the distance, but they weren't at the house yet, and it was thirty seconds later when the wall split apart and the two of you came tumbling out." She stopped, her voice choked with emotion.

Awkwardly Jessica put her arms around her mother's shoulders. "I'm so glad you were there," she said.

Mrs. Wakefield tried to smile. Her eyes filled with tears. "Thank goodness we were," she said, taking a deep breath. "I saw the fire from a distance, and I thought—I thought—" She shook her head quickly and hugged the twins tightly. "I'll spend the rest of my life being grateful that I was wrong."

Silently, arm in arm, the three Wakefields walked toward the spot where Eva's grave lay. Jessica noticed that the nearby grass was greener and lusher than she remembered, and the ground was smoother and more even. The tombstone sparkled in the sunlight.

The scattered daisies were gone, Jessica saw, and the whole grave looked somehow different. She strained to remember the horror she'd felt when she'd been playing hide-and-seek with Eva around this very grave. But the feelings wouldn't come back easily. "It's peaceful," she said aloud, listening to the wind gently shake the leaves on the nearby trees.

Elizabeth nodded solemnly.

Mrs. Wakefield blinked back tears. "I tried to forget Eva, but that was wrong," she said. "Maybe keeping people alive in your heart helps them rest in peace."

Jessica watched her mother place a bouquet neatly at the foot of Eva's grave. A bouquet of daisies, carefully cut and carefully arranged. As she did, one single small yellow petal peeled off its stem and drifted through the air into Jessica's hand.

It's an ordinary petal, Jessica thought, staring at the flash of yellow between her fingers. But she couldn't help shivering. It seemed eerie some-how, the way the petal just blew over to her. *There's still so much I don't understand. Like exactly how Eva Sullivan came to do the things she did . . . and how she managed to enter our dreams. . . .*

Jessica licked her lips.

And that's OK.

Bending down, she ran her fingers lightly over the inscription at the bottom of Eva's tombstone.

"May our daughter sleep at last in eternal peace."

"In eternal peace," Elizabeth whispered.

Jessica looked up, smiling. *In eternal peace.*

She stared off into the bright sunshine, thinking about Eva's brutal life and glad that after twenty-five years the inscription's wish had finally come true.

"I promise not to forget you, Eva," Mrs. Wakefield whispered.

And together they turned to leave.

What happens when Jessica and Elizabeth go on a double date—with twin boys? Find out in Sweet Valley Twins #101, TWINS IN LOVE.

Bantam Books in the SWEET VALLEY TWINS series.
Ask your bookseller for the books you have missed.